EX LIBRIS

VINTAGE CLASSICS

## JACK HILTON

Jack Hilton was born in the opening days of 1900 in Oldham, Lancashire. He served in the army during the First World War and, after a period of homelessness and working odd jobs, became an active member of Rochdale's workers' rights movement, where his rallying speeches led to a court order banning him from further speechwriting. Instead, Hilton turned to prose writing as an outlet, using stints on the dole to hone his immense literary gift and produce his autobiographical novel, *Caliban Shrieks*.

A chance encounter with an editor in 1934 led to Hilton's discovery and paved the way for a short, but dramatic, writing career that saw the publication of five books – including *Caliban Shrieks* – and which greatly influenced the course of political writing in British literature. In 1950, Hilton retired from writing and returned to his first trade, plastering. He died in 1983. The publication rights to Hilton's literary estate were long considered lost, until their discovery in 2022 allowed for the republication of his work.

ALSO BY JACK HILTON

*Champion*

*English Ways: A Walk from the Pennines to Epsom Downs in 1939*

*Laugh at Polonius; or Yet, There Is Woman*

*English Ribbon*

JACK HILTON

# CALIBAN SHRIEKS

WITH INTRODUCTIONS BY
Andrew McMillan and Jack Chadwick

VINTAGE CLASSICS

1 3 5 7 9 10 8 6 4 2

Vintage Classics is part of the Penguin Random House group of companies

Vintage, Penguin Random House UK, One Embassy Gardens,
8 Viaduct Gardens, London SW11 7BW

penguin.co.uk/vintage-classics
global.penguinrandomhouse.com



First published in Great Britain by Cobden-Sanderson in 1935
First published in Vintage Classics in 2024


This paperback first published in Vintage Classics in 2025



A CIP catalogue record for this book is available from the British Library

ISBN 9781784878764

Printed and bound in Great Britain by Clays Ltd, Elcograf S.p.A.

The authorised representative in the EEA is Penguin Random House Ireland,
Morrison Chambers, 32 Nassau Street, Dublin D02 YH68

Penguin Random House is committed to a sustainable future
for our business, our readers and our planet. This book is made
from Forest Stewardship Council® certified paper.

# Contents

# Introduction

Jack Hilton's decision to conjure up Caliban in the title of his novel makes a strange kind of sense when I think about what you're about to embark on reading. In one of his first speeches in *The Tempest*, Caliban speaks to Prospero:

> *For I am all the subjects that you have,*
> *Which first was mine own king; and here you sty me*
> *In this hard rock, whiles you do keep from me*
> *The rest o'th'island.*

Hilton describes his protagonist as 'my modern Caliban'. Given this, we might be moved to ask ourselves, what is kept from him, and by whom? On the hard rock of the country, who stys in the masses, who takes their freedom and their power from them? This long, experimental shriek is an attempt to move towards an answer.

★

Reading is so often a haunted pursuit. One sentence speaks to you, and suddenly other works, other writers, begin to echo from the cave walls of your mind. Other people emerge, Caliban-like, blinking into the harsh glow of your bedside light. *Love on the Dole*, Walter Greenwood's classic novel, appeared two years prior to *Caliban Shrieks*, in 1933; and just a few years before that there was the even more famous – infamous – *Lady Chatterley's Lover.* Two very different books, but ones from the same family, or perhaps the same community. Just as in *Lady Chatterley's Lover*, the dialect in *Caliban Shrieks* always arrives in reported speech, a more formal voice carrying us towards and away from the voices of the real people we encounter in the novel. Whereas *Love on the Dole* often situates us in one room, in one house, with one family, the novel you're about to read runs shouting down the street, trying to wake everybody up.

This novel is a conundrum that can only be answered by reading it. There is a narrative but not in any conventional sense; it's almost filmic in its sensibilities, or perhaps it anticipates the nature of episodic box-set TV shows. Each scene here could be a different, self-contained novel, shifting location and constantly oscillating between eccentricity and stark social realism.

The chapters themselves are poetic monologues; one of the most interesting questions arising from this novel is: who is being addressed within them? There's a sense of Hilton having a certain idea in his mind of whom a generalised reader of a literary novel might be; he speaks to them (to us) sometimes in anger, sometimes with disdain, sometimes as though we're part of the elite who is causing the conditions that are being shown. There's an odd sense throughout that the people who are so central to Hilton – the people in the pub, the ordinary soldiers, the wider community – aren't imagined as readers of the book. His imagined reader is Prospero, not Caliban.

You'll notice the direct, almost polemic nature of some of the observation – perhaps not something we're used to in the contemporary moment. The novel often speaks directly to us (that monologuing). It doesn't give its philosophical debates to characters to thrash out with each other; the political ideas of the novel are directed at the reader. 'Economy the damnable', it exclaims at one point. Beyond its politics, *Caliban* is a novel that is interested in the notion of what it is to leave and return to a place which seems to stay the same while the world around it changes; in the shattering, complex consequences of the war for a generation of men who returned broken, or who didn't return at all, and the younger ones who never went. As I write this I realise, of course, that there is nothing beyond politics.

In 2023 I was invited to visit Eton – the most famous private school in the country (if not the world), which counts amongst its illustrious alumni future kings and former prime ministers – to give a reading. I went out of a kind of morbid curiosity. What struck me most beyond the extravagance of privilege (the library at Eton holds one of the rarest original copies of the

*Gutenberg Bible*) and the period costume the young boys were forced to wear as though taking part in a permanent restaging of history, was the institutional memory of the place.

One of the first things I was shown when I arrived was the spot where Shelley had carved his name on a plinth. Later, I was taken to the wall where so many generations of young boys have sat to be photographed. Earlier that week I'd visited my parents, who still live in the same village I was born in, just on the outskirts of Barnsley. The school I went to in that same village is a Tesco Express now. I can't imagine that would ever happen to Eton. After I'd given my talk and was heading back on the train, which departed from just across the road from Windsor Castle, I was struck by a profound sadness which took several weeks to lift. I didn't see the point of anything any more. Arguments about so-called 'levelling-up', about redistributing funding and opportunities more fairly around the country, trying to expand the kinds of stories we hear and from whom we hear them – what was the point? Eton exists. It exists to carry forward its own institutional memory and influence into future generations. If most other people are at the whims of the tides of history and politics and the economy, then Eton steams ahead, not looking over its shoulder, creating the waves. Why do I mention this? The story of something like Eton, and the story of someone like Jack Hilton, seem interlocked somehow. 'The law of the loaf is the law of life', writes Hilton, 'without it one starves, with it one lingers.' Who holds the bread, in society, in publishing; what inequalities are already baked into our wider cultural conversations and narratives? Who gets to sustain? Who falls away?

On my journey home I changed trains in London to head back up to Manchester and found myself sitting across the aisle from two comedians, whose heyday had been in the late 1980s and early 1990s when they would tour and present light-entertainment shows on prime-time TV. They were telling end-of-the-pier jokes to each other and trying to make the carriage laugh. Occasionally someone trying to get to the buffet car would stop and linger, as though trying to place them. Somebody introduced themselves, but found they'd mistaken them for someone else of the same era. Some power is permanent, hewn into the rock of the nation, immovable except for the earthquakes of revolution or civilisational collapse. Some power, or stardom, is fleeting, can wax and wane, and so often the former power, that which is entrenched, gets to determine the latter. Who stays in the public eye. Who still gets read. Who still gets a seat at the table, when it comes to the serving of the bread.

Jack Chadwick will tell you more about the remarkable literary detective work and determination that has brought this novel back into the light, and more about why such an endeavour was necessary in the first place. Taking a step back, however, from this singular experience, it's worth reflecting on why this reissue is even necessary. Why wasn't this novel still in print? Why do certain writers need to be 'rediscovered' while other books endure? It is partly luck and happenstance, but it is also about someone who didn't have connections, who didn't have the footholds of privilege and security that prevent some of us from slipping down the ladder. This is Jack's story to tell – both Jacks. The reissuing of this book is the story of Jack Hilton's remarkable achievement of narrative and voice and vision, and Jack Chadwick's hard work and championing of a book that might otherwise have remained hidden and forgotten. I don't mean to speak over either Jack: if you are about to walk into Hilton's mind with Chadwick as your tour guide, I am merely at the door, collecting coats, nodding politely as you enter.

Jack Hilton was born and died in Oldham, just up the road from where I'm writing in my house near the Newton Heath & Moston tram stop. My ex-partner used to work in the H&M in the shopping precinct in Oldham town centre and sometimes I'd go to meet him after work, looking at the different Metrolink stops as I rolled past them. Failsworth, Chadderton, Westwood: how many other writers, and how many other stories might there be in these places? How can we ensure that we find them? That we hear them? How can we ensure that once we're listening, we'll keep listening? The stories of places like Oldham are the stories of the nation. This is just one example of that. Oldham exists! Eton exists! Writers like Jack Hilton keep falling out of memory. What is there to do, except persist, persist, persist.

Andrew McMillan, 2024

# Two Calibans

The difference between this and the first edition of *Caliban Shrieks* is that there are now two Calibans, both of us called Jack.

Nearly a century after Jack Hilton committed his original shriek to paper, it made its way to me from the inner recesses of a library in Salford. I – another working-class man, another Northerner, another Jack – saw in the corner of my eye the image of a skeleton, reaching out from a yellowing book jacket. For the rest of that day I sat and read, compelled to listen to what this skeleton had to say. When his story ended I felt desperate to know what happened next. What had become of this bloke, Jack Hilton, who'd drawn the macabre figure on the cover, labelled it 'me', and then proceeded to pour out his early life so completely, so poetically, into the pages behind it? Piecing together that answer set me on my own journey. A journey that I think of as my own shriek. The same tone, timbre and pitch as Hilton's. Just eighty-eight years later.

I discovered that while *Caliban Shrieks* – a masterpiece lauded by the likes of Auden and Orwell – had earned its author entry to the world of professional publishing, Hilton had eventually been forced out of writing. His class position imposed harsh limits on the literary legacy he could leave behind. This felt like finding a lost fourth act to *The Tempest*, wherein Caliban is reduced once more to serving Prospero. The result of the limits placed on Hilton was that his novels – some of the most strikingly brilliant literary works of their time – were boxed away: their author silenced, his words kept from his people, while many lesser literary voices, mediocrities with means, boomed.

*The Tempest* is the only Shakespeare play I've ever seen. My English teacher went to great lengths to sort a trip for my class to go and watch it at the Royal Exchange in Manchester. I am glad, not only because I don't think I could've passed my English GCSE otherwise, but also for the fact I probably would not have opened (or even come near) Hilton's novel had I not recognised the name of the creature on the cover. As I write this I am keenly aware of how so many working-class people – my friends and family – do not know their Calibans from their Prosperos and feel lost in the kind of writing formed around allusions to such a cast. I think, how easily I could have been them without that school trip. That the elitism of publishing kept Hilton in the role of Caliban, of outcast, even after he'd proved his brilliance across several great works, is an affront not just to Hilton, but to Hilton's kind, his class, our class. Prospero's daughter Miranda saw her father's slave as immune to 'any print of goodness'. The elites of publishing saw no good reason to keep Jack Hilton in print. Uneven scraps tossed to him in Rochdale from the publishers' big tables in London were not enough to sustain him. After each new book, however great, he was in the same position of having to beg around for his next contract. He slowly gave up.

Translating his talent into a consistent literary career proved too steep a challenge. A Wedgwood heiress working at Jonathan Cape, the publisher who had done best by him, summoned Hilton from Rochdale to Highgate only to refuse him the kind of multi-book deal that would have provided him the means to live securely from his words. 'The proletarian novel is dead,' she reasoned. A good friend, Eric Blair, was along as support for Hilton but even Orwell could not help his friend overcome the forces then stacked against the kind of proud, bold, creative working-class writing that Hilton had mastered. These forces were amplified by the subtle unease that disruptive, unconventional works like Hilton's brought to those thoroughbreds sitting comfortably at Imperial typewriters in the metropole, with the power to decide who could, and could not, write for a living.

Hilton returned to plastering. The money was better, and by then – the end of the forties – work was plentiful. In a way the retreat from a full career in writing saved him *as* himself. As a manual worker, a proletarian, it would be easier for him to live *by* his words – more important for a man like Jack Hilton than living *from* them. He was rightfully wary of how a literary career might warp him. 'Whenever I'm with the intellectuals I always feel they do not belong to my world', he wrote. 'With all their mentalised life they have had very little experience of living . . . they've been too sheltered, and too looked up to.'

If the cost of becoming a full-fledged professional writer would have been his stunning independence of thought, then he was happy, even in a way relieved, to stick with plastering. Which he did – with a deep care for a craft he loved. His hands went to work across Manchester for decades, beautifying houses. Much of his artisanship likely remains – he usually worked on big houses, that is, for people of the same class whose limited tastes had blocked him from a career as an author.

The enduring legacy of most other writers of the same generation as Hilton – the ones who got deals when he could not – is the landfill. Until his recent rediscovery, Hilton's legacy was his plasterwork: the reliefs, the finishes, the friezes of those Greater Mancunian mansions he had gone to work on. Not to mention the skills he passed on to his apprentice-learners and the subsequent craft of their younger hands. The union branches Hilton founded also must count for something. The better lives won by these chapters for their workers is a legacy Hilton, as one of the founders of the Lancs Plasterers' Union, more than shares in. This legacy in plaster suggests he was right to not really be that bothered about the rejections his writing career had knocked up against. His voice and image are protected forever from the garbling effects of 'mortgaged respectability'.

Nonetheless the fact that Hilton had been driven from writing on account of his class was hard for me to swallow when I had *Caliban Shrieks* in front of me, testament to his immense talent. That shriek of my own began to form. He should have been able to keep writing, had he wanted to. At one point he clearly did. The most heartfelt realisation, for me, in the saga of the second life of this novel – its rediscovery and the emergence of this new edition – is in finding that so many others share my indignation, my dismay over the treatment of a talent that should be celebrated throughout Lancashire and beyond.

Of course, as the Caliban of the text you are about to read would insist you know, being known and celebrated does not mean you are or were the best. How many more Calibans have toiled in complete obscurity to create great works? My shriek is Hilton's echo, loudest on this point. It is that of a second, junior Caliban, calling out to correct a wrong done to the first. But it has become a call to those many, many other creatures whose thoughts and voices remain ignored, even by themselves: people who will never receive even refusals, let alone offers, to express or create. Those taught to refuse our own thoughts before even composing them.

★

Like those other Calibans, Hilton could easily have not had any literary career at all. The hard-up, penniless one he did have was a triumph of chance. The fact it occurred is just as lucky for us, his readers, as it was for Jack himself; though it brought him little financial reward and a lot of stress.

In 1934, *Caliban Shrieks* came about through a sequence of flukes. The only intent was that of a kindly if underhand tutor who 'borrowed' one of Hilton's shabby exercise pads, which had been left behind at a night class. The tutor was a volunteer for the Worker's Educational Association. Hilton was forgetful of his books because these classes usually followed a day of hard graft or, if not, he would be fighting hunger in order to learn. The tutor sent the pad to a small, but brilliant, crusadingly modernist literary magazine, the *Adelphi*. What the tutor had discovered was the clamouring nucleus of *Caliban Shrieks*, which emerged full-throated a year later owing to the encouragement and connections of the magazine's people.

Hilton's shriek opens with a humble lie: 'You taught me a language, and my profit on't is, I know how to curse.' Really, our Caliban had taught himself the language of the masters, at a time when the Prosperos of the industrial world had run out of profitable uses for their servants. Cold and hungry, one of many workless men, our Caliban sheltered in Rochdale's only public library. Here he went 'learning me your language'. Working from the age of nine meant Hilton's only real education was his own brute effort here, in this desperate period of his early thirties (*the* early thirties).

What brought him to the library was anger at the hunger he and others were made to endure by the lack of work. Hilton and a few mates began to dream of resistance. Their first rough attempt at a political meeting brought only 'a little lad and a dog'. Their daily purpose was to improve, to win over Rochdale with orations against the town's hunger. They rushed 'from inarticulateness to eloquence, mastering the fluency of speech, the meaning of words, words, words'. Shakespeare, Marx, Lawrence.

Perfected, the riotous language of these Calibans, especially our Jack's, became too potent to go unchallenged. Hilton was marked a troublemaker and sent down by a magistrate, to HMP Strangeways. Upon release he was bound over, barred from speaking for his cause for three years. Pen and pad became the only outlet for the voice he'd learned to wield just as well as any rosette-wearing Prospero. I cannot think of any other writer with such a desperate, noble start to their use of English.

I'm writing this bit in a pub. The Sportsman's Arms, a Chadderton institution. A week ago I brought a journalist from the *New Yorker* here. Before that, I'd brought pilgrims from national print media, university professors, curators. Collectively reminiscent of a bad bar joke, x, y and z walk into a bar, so on. As a barman myself I've heard a lot of those. I wonder what the lasses behind this bar think of this weird parade.

I'm sitting here writing – pint, pad, biro – because this

was Hilton's local. His council flat is still here, a minute up the road. I found the address on his death certificate and came down to the pub because of that desperation I wrote of earlier, that need to know more about our Caliban.

My first visit I came with some handmade posters printed off at Central Library, a long shot. In greyscale, they asked if anyone remembered Jack Hilton. My number was on little pull-off paper tassels. Desperate.

It felt impossible that anyone would remember Hilton: a quiet bloke, no kids, dead for thirty-nine years. Impossible that he could have left a substantial enough mark on a local boozer for memories to remain after all this time. The fact that a regular in the Sportsman approached me that first visit about one of the posters before I'd even finished my pint was staggering. Her memories of Hilton were vague but she could tell me the names of his best pals, Bill and Brian. Bri had gone on drinking there for decades, long after Hilton's last orders in 1983.

I looked up Brian's address. It was just around the corner. Back to Chadderton a week later, I knocked on. No answer. I popped a note through the door. I'd later learn that the resident of the address was about to move out. Had I come a week later, Mary would, in the chaos of the move, very likely have never received my soggy note – another fluke. She emailed me back. Her beloved husband Brian had passed away the year before.

Mary was chuffed to receive my note through her letterbox about her old friend Jack. I went to visit her a few weeks after, in her new place. The first of many chats over custard tarts. Before his death, Jack used to come round to Mary and Brian's for his tea several times a week, eating with them and their two boys. None of the family had known that he'd ever been a writer, nor did they ever hear much about his tumultuous early life. Despite the great polemics of his youth, he was a listener at heart.

Mary is a brilliant, kind, immaculately presented Irish Mancunian. Old Ancoats through and through. Her 'fond memories of dear old Jack' record his peaceful, grandfatherly presence in the life of her boys. He'd sit and listen to them chattering about their days at school and, when entertainment was required at the dinner table, he'd whip out his pipe and blow smoke rings. If the lads needed even more distraction, Mary tells me he could blow the smoke *from his ears*.

Party trick, yes, but I did some research: only someone with badly damaged eardrums could pull smoke through them. Our Caliban's deformed ears could have been a byproduct of the pounding machinery of those mills he'd started in at eleven; or maybe the shells dropping on the trenches he'd been thrown into at seventeen; or the years of his twenties, wracked by war trauma, condemned to the loud drudgery of rock-breaking in 'the spike' (workhouses).

Mary and I chatted for hours about Jack as an older man. My favourite story is the fate of his beloved budgie. After Jack's death, Mary and Brian had inherited the little thing. They bought a new cage with all the trimmings. Within just a few days of Jack's passing, the budgie followed his master. Dead. The cause: the effects of nicotine withdrawal on its tiny anatomy. Caliban had loved his roll-ups. His flat walls were yellow. Home from the pub, I look at mine and crack open the window.

His poor loyal budgie made me realise – a doomed bird was probably not the only thing Jack had left for Brian and Mary's safekeeping. I wondered if Jack's literary rights had passed to the loving pair without their knowing he had ever written a thing. Using information from Mary I tracked down his last will. They had. I gave Mary the news along with a print-out of *Caliban Shrieks* that I'd spent weeks transcribing from the copy in Salford's Working Class Movement Library. She entrusted the rights to me. The one condition: I do my best to get her Jack back in print. This new edition is dedicated to the memory of her Brian, for the part he played in Jack's life.

The story of this novel's creation is every bit as beautifully quixotic as the man whose life it tells. The same is true of its return, its long-overdue second life. And I don't think it could have happened without a second Caliban to lend a hand. I am so immensely proud to have had that role.

Jack Chadwick, 2024

This newly reissued edition of *Caliban Shrieks*
is dedicated to Brian Hassall

'*Every work of art is a child of its age*'
Wassily Kandinsky

This book is a child of the 1930s and contains language or depictions that some readers may find outdated or offensive today.

Our general approach is to leave the book as the author wrote it. We are not endorsing its language or depictions; we are recognising that the book has literary or historical value. We encourage readers to consider the work critically and in its historical and social context.

# Caliban Shrieks

# Preface

CALIBAN IS A MAN YOU SHOULD KNOW WELL. 'A freckled whelp hag-born – not honour'd with a human shape.' He holds opinion about *his* rights; such foolishness he should overcome. 'Hag-seed, hence! Fetch us in fuel; and be quick, thou'rt best to answer other business,' than say, 'I must eat my dinner. This island's mine – which thou takest from me. When thou camest first, thou stroked'st me and madest much of me, wouldst give me water with berries in't, and teach me how to name the bigger light, and how the less, that burn by day and night; and then I loved thee and show'd thee all the qualities o' the isle, the fresh springs, brine-pits, barren places and fertile; cursed be that I did so – for I am all the subjects that you have, which first was my own king.'

I know the musings and tirades of my modern Caliban flout all the accepted rules of writing, but, 'You taught me a language, and my profit on't is, I know how to curse. The red plague rid you for learning me your language.'

I break from the personal to a diatribe against all and sundry but here is 'Neither bush nor shrub, to bear off any weather at all and another storm abrewing.'

You may not want to be disturbed by Caliban's inflated inflicted importance, still he is here. I give you his story, from infancy to infirmity, as clear as my feeble ability can arrange it for you. The jargon is one of the 'Clamorous Demagogue' for which there is no apology.

Yours, JACK HILTON

# Boyhood

I FIRST SAW LIGHT in the year nineteen hundred, most likely by chance, resulting out of what is possibly the over-indulged enjoyment of the sexes. It was, I am informed, a very snowy day (that may be the reason I am rarely cold). My Mother would be then twenty-five and Dad was ten years older. There had been five children previously and of course being one of fortune's favourites my birth came to pass in a back street in a smoky industrial town. Of the first five years I have little or no recollection, I suppose there were the usual things: measles, convulsions, and the eternal lung exercise of crying.

From about five I began to have contact with my species, and the thing I remember most was the cruelty of it. I lacked infant aggressiveness and as child life is composed of physical improvement, such as fighting, exercising, getting bigger and stronger, my absence of this natural drive to maturity made me the sport of the kids of the various alleys we were constantly moving in and out of. (You all know I presume that 'moonlights' were common events round about the '05 to '14.) Somehow I could never strike first and if I did defend, it generally stopped at that. This was quite the goods for the little tinkers, how they enjoyed the jungle freedom to sock me! I think the softy amongst a group of boys is grossly misjudged, what leatherings he takes, and he gets plenty, and ever there is a continued more in the offing. First the cock of the back does his stuff and then seeing how easy it is the second-raters take him on, so softy is lambasted by all and sundry. To use a sporting parlance: he becomes a chopping block. There is the utmost difficulty for him to get prestige; what is this prestige in infancy but the ability to frighten your man off? Reputation holds the fort as much in boyhood as in later life: get known as a scrapper and you often scrape through without a contest, get known as a softy and the hurly burly of opposition is greater than the local champion has to contend with. Fancy, softy is ever pummelled; receives; occasionally gives; but it is a hopeless defence against the champion of reputation. He is the hub that all fly at, the butt of all frolics. Still, conditions make the man and being the receiver-general hardens one for the future.

Now as to the conditions of living. Food? Bread and salt butter, tea and maybe half an egg for breakfast. Dinner? What an art there must have been in its deliverance to the table! Sometimes fish (this was fish necks, noted for their cheapness) with potatoes, and then pudding of stale bread and currants made into a batter and mildly roasted in the oven. Tea was like breakfast, minus the half egg and plus whatever was going cheap, savoury duck, London lettuce or bacon bits. What a job Ma had, stoking the hungry mouths of the household. Talk about the science of economy; meat, bones, brains of sheep boiled in a rag, the remnants of greengrocery, cabbage leaves, celery tops and the ever-filling vegetables – potatoes and swedes – these were the A B C's of a science bearing the name which is a blot on civilisation: Economy the damnable. Intermixed with the normality of such a home circumstance, there were periods of drab leanness, unemployment, the old man meeting Ma, the intuitive knowledge that the inevitable had once again happened, a smile belying the sad hopelessness of the situation; the eternal chase after the loaf of existence made more difficult by no wages. Rations cut, egg gone, treacle introduced; if anything, the change from just enough to less than what was needed became an accepted fact with us.

'Dad's on the Guardians' was how we summed it up. Little or no fire, clogs examined every night, tannings if there happened to be irons off, no lamp lit and all of us dumped into bed an hour earlier. Of course to balance this, now and again we had some rare treats. At Christmas (one of the few justifications for such things as churches) the nearby christian scrapers came out of their shell and stood treat for the poor of the neighbourhood, the policeman used to give out the tickets and what a morning we had, what a do! Snow cakes, mincepies, ham sandwiches – yes, real ham – Father Christmas himself used to deliver you a parcel of toffees and fruit and a toy, then you landed home crying because someone had trod on it and broken it.

Then there were the picnics about once a year in the summer. The carrier of the district would loan free his lorry, maybe two or three, planks would be thrown across them for seats, a bit of white calico was used for draping and away we went for a six-mile trip into the country.

What cheers at each new thing we saw! The better type of our parents would be with us, having walked, and would be plying us with anything we saw and wanted, such as fever-blossoms, dandelions, or buttercups. Easter too was a time of import. The peace egging had to be done, the inevitable scramble for the part of all-conquering Saint George and so downward via Slasher, King of Egypt, Black Prince, Hector, and Dr Quack to the ignoble Dirty Bett. None of us knew the symbolic significance of our various characters. Still by the numerous times we gave public evidence of our powers we became word perfect. Iron swords, coloured sashes, soot moustaches, the doctor's tall hat and the skirts of the Dirty Bett constituted the 'props' of our first association with drama. We were pukka strolling players. The nightly arguments as to policy, whether the few coppers should be immediately divided or allowed to be put by until Good Friday on which day the companies always wound up. Visions of an immediate joy, a bottle of pop between seven, and a halfpenny apiece, or the deferment and a good solid beano at the end. No set of seasoned matured advocates ever deliberated more seriously or more eloquently than the spokesman of each side. I am afraid the temptation of an immediate share-out generally won the day.

Now we will leave play and get down to school, the days of the strap, stick and uniformity, running away excused (occasionally of course). Cellulose collars (washable) and blackened clogs were the veneered hallmark, and just as indispensable to our education, as are now the pinstripe, spats, and horn-rims, to our present-day black-cloth imbeciles. One never dared to go to school otherwise, and, seeing matriculation was not in our curriculum, we must have some rigid type distinction.

Prayers came first and last, morn and afternoon. This added to the seriousness of being late with its aftermath of two strokes with the cane on each hand. Believe me, neither hair nor spit eased the pain, nor did the pulling back of the hand make the administerer forget how many you had had. The prizes always went to neatness. Parrotism ruled the roost. 'Say this after me.' 'Answer this after me.' The same old questions until we had by constant dunning the answers on the brain.

What impartiality we got for history! Stories about little drummer boys' valour, the minstrel boy and hearts of oak. The horrors of the Black Hole of Calcutta, the glory of Nelson and Drake's game of tiddlywinks – or was it bowls? Needless to say we were told Bill Adams won the battle of

Waterloo and our teachers conveniently forgot to mention about America gaining her independence.

What a fighting chance we were given to understand the happenings of world significance – it was not a dog's chance. It worked out this way. 1st: Heaps of God; 2nd: England first – the world nowhere; 3rd: Blatant swagger; one good innocent honest Christian blue-eyed English schoolboy equalled twenty infidel Japs (Ju Jitsu being barred of course).

Thus equipped with psychic sagacity we entered the labour market as half timers, stimulated to enterprise with the story of Dick Whittington and a book called 'Her Benny' covering Silas Hocking's philosophy. (How the devil some of us have mastered the vagaries of horse-racing form since, beats me.)

Six o'clock in the morning, dark and chilly, a bit of tommy in a red handkerchief and a breast of good intent. The myth of work being a recreation faded the first morning and the grit of a super-English brand was solar-plexused within a week. Talk about Indian summer being a beautiful vision, it was a blasted reality in a cotton mill. Four walls, caged captivity, hellish noise, wheels going round, motion, speed, punches up the posterior to acclimatise you (golly, Mr Millowner's daughter, marry me quick before I lose heart!)

What a blinking sandwich, mill and school plus homework! – with the baby brother sticking its jammy paws on your dictation. Neatness, where is thy sting? The schoolboy complexion turning to a corpse-like bleach! But as a tonic we could now smoke a woodbine, fellow-like, around the corner and so make ourselves paler. We even had greater privileges: the more daring could demonstrate their growing ripeness by expletives not learned at school. Society showed its interest in you the first week by the factory doctor sending you home; no, not for good, but until you put a flannel on. Half-time system, how many bow legs have you made? little puny legs shuffling along up hill at early morn, then bearing a doffing box plus a tired body. No wonder the comedians of the day made the Lancashire lad a skit; still it was a tragic one. What a price to pay for prestige; cotton the world and ruin the child! I was unbritish, got rebellious and, after a leathering from the jobber, ultimately fired as hopeless, much to my future benefit. Now, reader, let me slip two years. Take for granted the various blind alleys I travelled to take home a few shillings weekly. Errand boy to a type that had lost their manhood, born to be men, doomed to die grocers.

Oh that extra errand five minutes before finishing time and the call round at Mrs Brown's just before starting time, plus making you the human dishcloth and char hand! Despite this I want you to imagine me fourteen and a half years, just being fired for celebrating Shrove Tuesday on Ash Wednesday and after the usual beating at home and Ma's usual lecture, setting out once again on the road of misadventure, still determined to conquer the apostate within me and be a model of the do-your-best type.

The war was just on, folk were looking upon it as a picnic (how typically British). Six or seven reservists had gone up. What glory each of those households possessed.

I turned washers, now having been apprenticed. Gradually conditions of employment were improving, and, to make us diligent, piece-work was introduced. Many were the times I took my gross of washers to the store room, had them booked and stole back with them under my bib. Such were the results of my earlier christian training. Still it was a time when youngsters were being needed and pandered to; anything was right so long as we would wade into our work. As this dawned on me, my suppressed hatred of the brow-beating foreman class, from whom I had received so much callousness, took concrete expression; I belted the old foreman and attempted to show my truculence by leaving, but alas, the liberty of the subject during time of war made the task a difficult one. The matter was settled by the firm and my old Dad coming to agreement. (Incidentally it meant a rise in my screw.) After twelve more months of this four-wall association with the blue-overalled aristocracy I vomited my prison sickness, dashed to liberty and King Sol, so putting the onus of bringing me back on the firm, for the authorities were apparently too busy to bother about me, heaven bless them.

After that the open air only was good enough for me. So I honoured the local railway company with my services. Talk about engineers being perpetual repeaters, railwaymen are such slow plodders. What a lot! the Hodges of industry, elephant mobility but likewise men of strength. Traditions of little money and long hours, everlastingness, ever there always. Men of large output but it took a long time. The hand winch, the human lugging of cases, bales and sheets (politely termed pocket handkerchiefs). What is not done today will be done tomorrow and there is always Sundays to pull up the work that is behind. Double rupture was their industrial disease. Still, behind all this I believe the companies were guaranteed a fixed dividend by the Government that paid anything within reason to their friends for patriotism.

Wages were not as high as elsewhere because the adults could never leave except by joining the army. They were exempted and so had to lie down. Their country after 16 months of this 'picnic' was needing them to stick to their post in England; it was better than being shot at by some incompetent foreigner. I was by now developing a form of judgement of men and other things, a sort of idea was being born that kidology ruled the roost. All the tied-up indispensables wanted to go and knock stuffings out of the baby killers and women rapers, but noble duty made them deny themselves the discomforts. (Still the blinking conchy was given the bird by all.)

God save the King, anti-Germanism, fight to the last man (with exemptions for my trade, or over my age) was the stuff to give them. How Mr Keep-your-feet-warm, whom I had always worshipped as a sort of tin god, filled me with the importance of his convictions. Oh what a sorrow it was to him that he was too old to bathe his nice warm smug complacent respectable feet in the blood bath of the twentieth century. How I would soon be old enough to defend him and me six hundred miles away from home. He was overfed, bull-necked and beef-fed during times of national shortage, nobly doing his duty – watching the clouds roll by. What an interest he had in this war for humanity, buttonholing all and sundry with his patriotic zeal.

Of course he was only one of many of the same kidney. I listened to our Primrose Leaguer, with his imperialist equatorial corpulence showing him to be well over forty-five. My powers of analysis of rhetoric being dormant, his honesty was beyond dispute, and as a voluntary recruiting sergeant, he was a howling success.

Oh wonderful tripe known as eloquence, how powerful art thou over the Henry Dubbs of time! Honour, duty, service and sacrifice became words of magic inspiration; hallowed be their names. How I licked it up! (Since then I have learned what Falstaff says of honour.)

Added to this nightly travesty was the martial accompaniment of military bands, the adoration showered on the kilted pipers made one envious, the eulogy and public appreciation of the early D.C.M.'s all helped towards the collapse of the youthful mind.

It had to be done, there was no escape, the H.V. St Claires

fed us with their swinging jingo ditties; so it was that many of us were drawn in as voluntary infants to hang the Kaiser.

Played to the station, at the district barracks first barrage from a peppery colonel, given a regiment, a night at home, introduction to a tart, off the following day for training.

Service, honour and duty – didn't the old depot sweats know their meaning! All the money our parents and friends gave us, they fleeced from us with rapidity under the cloak of fatherly advice. Vocabulary, wonderful, marvellous, all of a colourful and sensuous kind, intermixed with an odd word or two here and there from old English. What had the Y.M.C.A.'s against this man's meat, pukka soldier stuff of the wet canteen? It was here that I learned the properness of promiscuousness. Oh with what we were told about the pox, really the poxed were inflated with a halo of consequence. A visit to the latrine with its canvas surround for privacy was quite an experience, an examination of the bowl of prevention, condies, roused one to inquisitiveness. This to us immature innocents abroad was getting one's teeth into understanding proper.

Forming fours, knowing left leg from right, more robotism, platoon work, and battalion treks over country were thc means of hardening and building one up to strength so that you can live to be ninety if not shot.

Here again – service, honour, and duty – the weak and soft were well looked after. The last man or biggest duffer always had to do it again. The bloke warned for a fatigue, if he was conscientious, turned up and the corporal would make a mental note of his willingness, so booking him for regular treatment. Still this home training was not bad if you learned the ropes, of which scrounging was a fine art. One must never be a 'can'*; never complain; dodge the column; work the whole bag of tricks and keep out of the mush.

Pull the M.O.'s for a dose of light duty now and then, drop the sergeant a pint, but only at a time when he most needs it, the day before pay is due.

Honour, service, and duty.

Take an interest in sport, put that extra bit of pep into it, be athletic and your other faults would be overlooked, get a reputation, get well past the rooky stage, use your napper, cultivate a decent curse – what blasted camouflage is this thing efficiency! Get on with your bragging, know how to gamble, when to make the sky the limit and when to act the policeman. Honour, service, and sacrifice; when I was seventeen I knew you as being as double darkly dyed as Iago.

Though officially I was considered to be eighteen and six months, humanity then decided you could not be shot at until you reached the age of ripeness, nineteen. So having passed the necessary training, fired my course, I was put on the staff to fill in the waiting period. A job in the stores, under an old hand, a quartermaster with a physique that had gone pop, but with cranium equal to the average general's. I

* Can=mug=fool.

did the work and he did the twisting. Weighing the maggy tea and sugar, counting the loaves and jam, disposal of same on basis of head rate of companies and proportionate ounces of the needful. This for the cook-house, that for A company, No. 1 platoon, and so forth. I often wondered why my quartermaster was so popular with the ladies, a lump of fat under the scales made up for the valued commodities he gave to the sweet sugared dames. Nothing at a loss, I being adaptable did the same by placing still another lump of fat to kid the corporals that they got their just fund of weight.

Still, virtue brought its own reward. I refused promotion and the aged home service Colonel collared me to look after his and the adjutant's mares. My word, didn't I drop on velvet! two titts to look after and exercise, two officers who dithered at the thought of having to mount them, what a break for me! I filled the bill naturally; after an odd kick or two, me and the mares were as a triple affinity, until my time to do the needful abroad arrived.

Polishing buckles, dubbing leathers, currying, brushing and grooming generally. 'Do you want your mares Sir?' No, not today, was always the reply: never an admission they were windy, and were full of envy of me riding them all over the show.

Sailing through space at a full gallop, getting accustomed to the awkwardness of a slow trot, taking a hedge or a gate at full belt. Oh! it just suited, all this heaven, and they never dared get near the bridle. Like all good things it came to an end; I was placed in the lot for the next draft. Another fortnight's hardening, one or two all-night skirmishes, sent home for ten days, then back to the mixings, being three days absent (of course that was usual). Then what a hustle: fresh kit, balmorals, webbing equipment, and YO HO! a pay book, disc and lanyard. On the eve of departure you helped yourself gratis to all the wet canteen possessed, next morning the old Colonel gave us his blessing, the sky pilot prayed for our salvation, we were bunged with iron rations and bond hooks, fell in and marched to the station, filled with the spirit of the ages.

Honour, service and sacrifice.

# The Picnic

THE ARMY WORKED on a slogan 'One Volunteer was worth ten pressed men': that was why we were placed twelve in a carriage and the door locked. There we remained from 6 a.m. to midnight, travelling due south. Then true to the honour of duty, passed through a strong cordon of military police and found ourselves deposited in those big houses (formerly they have been for boarders) facing the sea on the front at Folkestone. There was no pressure, mind you, but nothing was left to chance against your cutting adrift. There the bottom shelf (floor) was your kip, and with gunfire (char, otherwise tea) at 5 a.m. all were, though stiff, completely astir.

Linings up, stand easy's and shunnings helped to while away the time before embarkation. Oh Mr Cinema Packer, you should have been there, how they crowded the flower of England's youth on two wee boats beats me. Tramp, tramp, tramp, a never ending stream of fellows seemed to disappear. Once they got past the gangway (I learned afterwards) they disappeared down into the hold of the ship, packed jam tight, without light or ventilation. I was lucky, got a place on deck with more room to spew in. Each of us, passing the gangway, was given a lifesaver, it appeared to be a bit of white rag with pockets containing a few handfuls of corkdust. No doubt it was scientifically designed to be an efficient utilitarian expedient in case of need.

What yarns I had heard about the significance of the white cliffs of Dover, the pathos associated with their disappearance and such sob stuff, never entered into my experience. I only noticed the discomfort associated with the struggle that took place to lean on your mate and so relieve the strain of packed massed weight.

Eventually we did lose sight of Dover's cliffs, soon to see the outline of the French coast: what a contrast, umpteen transports packed with soldiers, all hooting for first right of way. Cheers of recognition and counter cheers, from ships all in turn unloading their human freight. Oh indeed, great individual, where is thy personality, what if your Dad is the big drummer in the Salvation Army, you are now one of many sick and hungry blokes wondering what is the next carry-on.

A long trek through smelly untidy streets, with mounted patrols at all turnings, on and on until eventually you pass through some barbed wire and you are at the Boulogne base. The sorting out process, roll call, put to your tents, twenty-two where there is only room for eleven – eventually the day passed. Owing to compactness you use your right boot for a chamber pot, emptying it under the flap of the canvas. No mother's pap, no benedictions, just the nightly grunt of shut-eye and 'A Soldier's Farewell'.

The next day: kit inspection, also health inspection during which the medical officer walks past, after you have been standing half naked for about an hour, and up to dinner time you fill in the void by being kept busy falling in and falling out. Then comes the big event, gas test, fullpack, march through the town, the residents – mostly old men, women and children – seem to have no interest in you; no doubt it is to them a daily occurrence, this stream of khaki is now commonplace. The women seem to possess a juvenile slenderness. The distant left of the town seems to be the west end, its architecture is pleasing. On and on, puff blow puff, left, left, right, left, no halting and lo! just as you are feeling creased, there is a brow as big as the heavens. What a stiffener; eventually you reach the top, you pass the staff headquarters, turn into a field, fall out and drop down dished. When you resume your composure, you are given an explanatory lecture. Thuds or duds (shells) may be gas, likewise vapours, fogs, or the smell of pineapple, always be on the alert for the hooter or whistle warning, never get fluttered, put on masks automatically and by numbers.

The practical performance is gone through of placing mask to face in a stipulated manner many times, then you are fit to enter the gas chamber. This happens to be an empty hut with a rail running through the middle, you proceed up one side and down the other in single file. Then you are allowed to saunter about the field. Then come the surprises. You have been told to be on the alert for light-sounding thuds, the smell of pineapple, and tears in the eyes. Crikey! don't the testers keep you busy, wherever you go there is some cause for donning the mask, if you are not smart you get unpleasant reminders, your breath goes, tears come, and you are coughing and spitting while the tester is laughing like blazes, reminding you what you should have done to prevent getting caught. Then comes the grand finale, of marching, doubling, and running like lunatics with the old bag adding to your difficulties of breathing. You thank your trainer for the gruelling, for it gives one confidence in the fact that one can live and survive though half-suffocated. Back to the base, just about dead beat, the overcrowded tent seems like paradise and one sleeps the sleep of the just.

After a day or so of messing about, your chance comes to get away. Crowded into a passenger train, minus panes in the windows, with the upholstery looking as though it had been chewed up, the lavatory stinking like a flax field, away we go.

Yes, go and stop, generally stopping. After travelling a dozen miles or so, we get transferred to covered vans and settle down to it. All have their backs to the sides, with legs fully stretched on the floor. By some kind of magic an old bucket is procured and a jerry (fire) is made. What a pleasure! Still the smoke from it makes you doubt its success but after such a brainwave and accomplishment one would be ungrateful if he objected to such a trifle as smoke. Some have blankets out, trying to sleep, some walking about in limited space up and down the centre, and others watching minutely through a slit in the door the dim outlines of whatever's outside. 'Go and stop' still rules the day. Fortunately with every stop someone scampers to the engine driver for hot water to make tea, out of what seems to be a tablet made of donkey-stone. I get called to one corner of the van by Corporal B. who has an idea, but he also has stripes so someone must put his brainwave into practice. Scout at all stops for scrounge (grub) was the idea.

Four of us drop out and despite drawing a blank on the first and second places the train stopped, the third proves successful. We are alongside of a goods train and, opening a wagon, there is bacon, yes, bacon. Out come knives in a flash, half a roll is collared in a dooda, a short sprint and we are safe back.

Songs break out, the fire is given a bit more fillip, out comes a dixie lid and the atmosphere assumes the homely aroma of sizzling bacon. What a feed, what a stroke of luck.

The train keeps going and stopping, we keep getting in and out for wood and boiling water, some are drowsy, some in song, some gradually snoozing, snoozing off, all getting cold and stodgy. Daylight is breaking, then eventually Poperinghe is reached. What is there in a name? Surely though I had never heard of it before, the subdued voice that uttered the name spoke volumes, for it signified the abandonment of hope for all who alight. The last link with safety, booze, and civilians.

Out of the vans all drag themselves, we all fall in, making a line as level to the eye as a corkscrew; left turn, forward, and quick march to some corrugated iron huts.

A wash and some grub, then a bit of go-as-you-please housey-housey, crown & anchor or tossing. What a fascination there is in gambling! What a lingo the bankers possess in crown & anchor, all of which is necessary to draw and keep their punters.

Loudly sings the thimble rigger, 'I'm Billy Fairplay, all the way from Holloway, never been known to run away. The sky's the limit, put down your dollops of dung and I'll pay you out in buckets of dysentery. You come here in rags and go away in motor cars. Shove it down thick and heavy. All paid-All-played and away we go again – up she comes with the best of luck – ther's two jolly mud hooks and a good old Kimberley.' So the day passes. We have been awaiting instructions as to future movement. Night comes, some are drunk, some have won a franc or so, others are skinned. After a row or two, quietness eventually reigns, giving chance for reverie to the minds so disposed; they can now wonder as to the whys and wherefores of the stone of philosophy.

I for one did not dwell on the conundrum, being soon in slumber.

The next day saw us on the move, we were going up the line – some said here, some there, no one seemed to know where. On and on we kept marching, singing 'Wash me in the water'.

# Hanging the Kaiser

THE MOON WAS LIT UP like a brilliant silvery disc, clouds of silvery puffiness lie around it. We see the silhouette of a building jutting at the corner. On approach it shapes itself into an old farmhouse flying at its peak a red cross. It happens to be a dressing station. We shelter momentarily and lo! there is, near enough to tread upon, the stiff cold forms of what was once two glowing breezy youths. So still and awry dead. The moon made their faces a bile-lit green. This was the first knock on my cranium of war's ignobility. We pass on, eventually being located by our guide. Poor chap, what a mess! stammering and all shakes, one of God's children who had been reduced to a hopeless lump of shocks and he was still leading reliefs through to others.

Under his guidance we cross a road in groups hurriedly, each group having made its spurt, he leads the way and single file we follow. From him come all whispers of direction and warnings, each one, passing the word on, to whomever is behind.

'Duckboard missing, jump it', 'Crouch low here', and such like precautions. Humour is added to the situation, by many who cannot conform to the procedure of follow-my-neighbour.

Some, when the moon has failed us, due to some cloud blotting it out, fall off the duckboards and go knee-deep in mud. Then we hear army language – Germans or no b—— Germans. Eventually we reach the reserve trenches. Here we are full of wonder, doubt, funk and camouflage bravado. What is it like? Well to be frank it is a glorified bit of navvying, about two small yards wide, the same in height and stretching irregularly as far as you need bother about. It has three courses of sandbags on the top. Every now and then there are cuttings which lead to the front-line trenches. Every movement is one of change, from lit-up sky to sudden gloom; this is caused by Verey lights bobbing up down like balls from a Roman candle. Our time comes to relieve those in the front line, so we get a glimpse of them. What has happened to them? They are jumpy, haggard, dirty, and semi-shocked. Phantom-like, yet possessing a stiffness born of cold and jaded numbness. Each, though unshaven and dishevelled, has a face that seems bleached. They pass us with a trudge and a permanent crouch, we fancy we hear them in the distance. Clatter, clatter, clatter, their heavy boots sound on the wooden battens. Slowly it appears to die away; they are gone, we are left. What awaits us?

It so happens that our baptism can be covered by the term 'all's quiet'. Oh so quiet: so uneventful: rats, rain, Verey lights, observation balloons, machine-gun fire with the regularity and softness of pneumatic drills, bombardments every now and again over our heads, on to the artillery behind us. Shrapnel above us dropping its numerous lumps of social blessing. 'Fountain of love our hope is in thee, the hope of the world is love.' No philosophy about that stuff, no symbolic significance, just a present from one set of civilised humans, to fellow humans who have been so cowardly as to dig themselves in.

What are we puny things, mortals in a ditch, each armed with a rifle? just a few of the million pawns similarly placed in a stupid stunt. Dug in, the relatively passive, incapable of functioning, being just there, firing feeble shots into space. The line that saves our mothers and sisters from rape and such like? Don't we soon realise that the big fellows, the machines, are winning or losing the war! We are just there to suffer neurotic shocks, inhuman physical hardships, become lousy but stay there until relieved – maybe never return. What room is there for courage; dug in? Mechanics doing the warring, you helpless, an exposure amounts to suicide – all this training, these cross guns for hitting a bull's eye and you are just there – yes, just there – a line of men, each side letting the other know you are there, dug in.

Hours like days, days like weeks, a week like eternity, and so at last relief comes and away we go, trudging and bent, stiff and cold, haggard and lousy, stammering and nervy, away from this official quiet spot. Out of it we are, washed and underclothes changed, clean but still lousy. The lice are the active serviceman's comrades and are still with us, but a dozen or so of our mates are missing.

Gradually we become men again, get down to 'housey-housey' again, the only blinking frost is the nearness to being 'dug in' again. In and out we go, sometimes quiet, sometimes not, here and there new faces, old ones left behind. What's it for? How long yet? Who's going next, what a bloody game! Honour, Service, Sacrifice, as a Falstaff would say: 'Can honour set-to a leg? no: or an arm? no: or take away the grief of a wound? no: Honour hath no skill in surgery, then? no. What is honour? a word. What is in that word honour? What is that honour? air. A trim reckoning! – Who hath it? he that died o'Wednesday. Doth he feel it? no. Doth he hear it? no. 'Tis insensible, then? yea, to the dead. But will it not live with the living? no. Why? detraction will not suffer it: – therefore I'll none of it: honour is a mere scutcheon: and so ends my catechism.' Honour the shibboleth of rhetorical fiddlesticks. What honour had we on March 21st 1918? Five hours of fog, gas, cannonade, then attacked by mass hordes of beastly blondes. Dug in, yes, but not invincible, put on the run by overwhelming odds. Yes, British pluck on the run, demoralised, licked to a frazzle, from orderly retreat to a panic; yes, a panic born out of the hellish attack, too much for any human endurance. Civilisation, religion, what beastly tricks you get up to. Bow your heads in shame. 'What a piece of work is a man, how noble in reason, how infinite in faculty, in form and movement how express and admirable, how like an angel, in apprehension how like a God.' Bill, dear boy, you must have turned over many times during this madhouse lunacy.

# Happy Days

BACK WE CAME DRIBBLING HOME in penny numbers. Home-townism, twenty-nine shillings on the dole. A glorious future when things had settled down; everybody was good to one another, a 'bon homme' friendship prevailed; mutual condolences and sympathies were reciprocated. Any of the lads who did anything wrong, who overstepped the mark a little, was forgiven, a second chance for all was the chivalrous air. The war was responsible for these idiosyncrasies! – all that was needed was a little time to settle down in. Morality would reassert itself, killers and diggers would adjust themselves to domesticity and industry.

The fat stay-at-home tin gods had tact; they smiled and beamed at us all. John Barleycorn flowed with refreshing sweetness through the mouths of the shining pumps. England returned to its sunny radiance of hope and glory. In this prophesied return to sanity, what days of happiness we had! They may not have been parlour-like, but still their memory is very sweet. Billiards, booze, contrasts of how each had fared, quite a group fraternity of association sprang up. The dear old ladies of the wartime welfare canteens carried on and loaded us with bun and tea hospitality. After getting fed up with draughts and ludo, or having a sing-song and knocking the piano about, we used to slyly creep away and climb the stairs to vacant and out-of-bounds rooms for some of our old-time recreation. We would there play cards, and only drop out of the school when we had no money. Many were the times when we would be so absorbed in our enterprise, that we forgot the place had long since closed. Nothing daunted, we would play on and at a late hour make our evacuation from upstairs via the window and down the ivy.

Oh that we could now return to such abandonment and audacity. We had afternoons of football matches, with picked sides. Running, jumping and all kinds of physical combat were indulged in. What happy days, the days permitted and condoned by the governing class as the settling-down period. I have a fleeting recollection amid this, of the first election I had that magnetic thing the vote, that wonderful all-power thing by which working men rule the land, whereby I was equal to all men, and the choosing of our governors was in my power. It was my first taste of the rotten game; I did not think it was rotten then, every speech made was genuine then to me. Rhetoric, pitching the tale, those final perorations all got home on my baby dullwittedness. 'We have won the war, we will make the peace' versus 'No reparations' seemed to me to be the issue at stake. Gallantry and British patriotism versus cowardice and conscientious objectionism seemed to be the two combating groups. Peculiarly, I was a freak in their midst, a silver-badger supporting with vote and energy labour pacifism. Oh yes, there was a reason; as a kid I'd had many pastings for carrying the coloured favours of socialism, Dad happened to be one, so I could not go over to the blue bloods.

Nevertheless politics were to be the school whereby I grew a little out of my ignorance. At political meetings one could sit, smoke and listen, even learn. I went to many, the habit grew, partisans of all sides were flooring, orally, the be-all and end-all of their opponents' policy. The better the speaker the more I liked his policy. What lumps of clay are we in our ignorance to the practised orator. How they got us to accept them as the heaven-sent saviours of humanity, now, beats me. 'Hang the Kaiser' brought down the house then; 'Make Germany Pay' was another good winner; and a promise of good things for everyone capped the lot.

'Vote for me and I will pull you through' was the tune we liked them to sing. To meet that popular demand each side vied with each other in singing, 'Its all for the working man' (afterwards the stage comedians took it up as a stock joke). All questions were alike in substance, 'What will you do for me?' Every candidate outbid his opponent in his determination to give the outraged and long-suffering holder of the vote, the moon. The drum of Parliament's purpose was to give promises to all.

The Labour man had one big card up his sleeve, which he generally pulled out effectively. Says he: 'You, the workers, are the most exploited class in society. You are the greatest of all men and all the products of the Earth, Sun, Moon, Stars, even the stars of seventh magnitude, should be yours. Send me and I will fight until I am throat-hoarse, on your behalf, sitting on the floor of the House of Commons.' Every talkative meddler, with thrust and ambition, was a Labour candidate, dying to emancipate the downtrodden. On the other side the successful suckers, and those with idle moments, were equally ready to represent their fellow Britisher at Westminster. Opportunism and a cushy job versus ornamentation and desire for social prominence about covered the bag of them in my later disillusioned opinion.

As you know, 'The old nobility of blue bloods', the winners of the war, won the election and set about the job of putting the world and the British working class on velvet.

# The Renaissance

HAVING BEEN AWAKENED BY LISTENING to the politicians, I developed a thirst for anything that was going by the way of lectures; even sermons became tolerable at times. One school in particular then captivated me, those fanatical highbrows of futurism, the cleaners of society, the formers of character, the builders of a new race. I read their works, 'Race Culture or Race Suicide', 'The Case for Eugenics'. Their statistics appealed. I found my Saleebys, Rintouls, and young Darwins. I read of their progress in many American States. They impressed me with their case against booze and immorality. The necessity of sterilisation, segregation and restricting the indulgencies of the inefficients, the half-wits, the epileptics, the criminal-minded, the dipsomaniacs. Even the strong but purely physical became a menace with their dominant naturalism of procreation.

Their eugenic idealism hit me so hard that I decided to accept it practically. I examined myself from their eugenic standard, I soon found my incompetence, accepted the fact of my inferiority, realised it would be criminal to burden society with any or many little pasty-faced dullwits, so therefore examined the groups of restricted liberty I'd better place myself in. I was moral for a man of my low station, so could not be placed in a male home for drunkards, kleptomaniacs or epileptics. I was neither syphilitic or gonorrheic, just one of the multitude of ineffective useless undesirables strutting my burdensome self on a world intended only for the intelligentsia of culture. I had like many of my class been accidentally born into the world by the chance of ignorance, and the only decent thing I could do was to see that I played no part in multiplying the vast hordes of flotsam and jetsam who annoyed, upset and tended to impoverish the super select race of oligarchic proportions.

I must do something – I have it, vasectomy, just a minor operation, no external mutilation, but freed from the responsibility of fatherhood. Off I went, thinking every medical man was a eugenic fan. I thought they would fall over themselves to do the job. The first listened, thought I had gone potty, told me not to have such a filthy mind, showed me the door and gave me a look unlike a Saint would give a leper.

Finding the average practitioner too busy attending confinements to muse about eugenics, I struck out and walked into the den of a St John Street specialist. He beamed, was conciliatory, found out I'd a guinea, took it off me, told me I still owed him another, then for eugenic treatment gave me a mile-long quotation from Hamlet about abnormal gloominess.

I, thanks to reading, feared rottenness and big families, I knew celibacy was unnatural; the Malthus school of moral restraint was impossible, the attraction of street-corner Aphrodites was dimmed by the knowledge of their possible uncleanliness. The clash between the desires of nature and the apprehension of fire has made a permanent sourness to my Falstaffian sensualness.

Other disabilities I derived from these people of good intent (eugenists): they were a disinclination to be fixed in unhealthy surroundings. The model workshop, the worker's cot, the street of civic pride, became dowdy, germ-infested, condemned, and places to avoid. Yet, to add to the irony, I being a conditioned being, was economically held fast to these environs of unhealthiness. I saw their inadequacies, how the workshop filled the lungs with dust, how the smoke hid the sun from the streets and back-to-back houses of home sweet home, how they had bad sanitary arrangements, filthy sinks and damp foisty-smelling walls, with little or no drainage; in fact everything opposite to the standards needed for bare decency and hygiene.

Still man struggles on, books can be read, despite the din of the neighbour's gramophone, and the healthy lustiness of many screeching kiddies. Great pages of philosophy, science, history, and antiquity, written by men of all times, could be got from the libraries and by this method, at least, minds could be in communion with those whose environments were opposite.

It is from these I got a rough cynical bite into the trousers seat of banality. I had suffered much from my lack of erudition, had often been made the butt of the petty supercilious wits. I was unabashed, undaunted and condemned everyone. Readers, dreamers, parasites or work-animals, damn you. Hermaphroditic, double-sexed, God and mammon Non-Conformists, or Coriolanus bloods of blue, damn you too, especially the bulk of you. Civilised lumps of protoplasm with plus-four adornments and horn-rimmed impediments, damned be you as well. Civil certainly, but what's it all mean? Understrapper servility, holy-Michael piety, meekness, watch your step, every step, a life sentence to orthodoxy. Stupid pawns, robots, unimportant pigmies, bowing, scraping, never getting within a thousand miles of the oligarchy you serve.

Completely estranged from the mad enjoyment of Bohemia, murder, fanaticism, chained permanently to obedience and a consideration of your overseers, all of you overseen and paying the blackmailer's price, which is the bankruptcy of expression. Sucked dry by the tenacious tentacles of the octopus of civility. To use a good old Lancashire term 'You're Daft.'

Three score and ten years, then, sans everything; your Malvolian superciliousness, your beastly blondes of toil are all gone, nappo finni. Despite your subterfuges, supermanisms, greatness, voluntarily or otherwise, you are doomed to enter 'that undiscovered country', call it what you will, Paradiso, Purgatorio, or Inferno. So be it, damn you, you mortals that are as God's angels, you monstrous cullions, charlatans, and pedantics. Damn you all again, and may we each retain our mutual contempt. 'For the souls of animals doth infuse themselves into the trunks of men, for their desires are wolvish, bloody and ravenous.'

It was with such vituperations I used to lash myself and soliloquise and then feel much eased.

Still my jaundiced outlook made it impossible to stick to localisation. Rebellion came upon me, and I, intended for industry, for being a clean-nosed respectable god-fearing climber, surrounded by grime, strict discipline, crowding and the dignity of labour, took to the road, the open road, with visions of liberty, freedom, air, sun, and health. Damn the methodical work game, damn the churchwarden and his tray for the eternal threepenny bit, hang the football coupons. The road, nomadness, no shaving, no soft-soaping to respectable city fathers, no accepting of patronage from bilious old Victorians of the duffer brand, no more ambition, no set purpose, just drift, drift, drift, complete scope for nannygoat whimsicalness, and eternally the 'captain of my soul'.

# The Tramp

*'There is not in the wide world a valley so sweet*
*As that vale in whose bosom the bright waters meet.'*

TOM MOORE

*'If Moore was like me with no*
*brogues to his feet,*
*Lying down in a barn and having*
*nothing to eat,*
*Getting up in the morning to face a*
*cold driving sleet,*
*He wouldn't give a damn where the*
*bright waters meet.'*

THE TRAMP

THE LILY-PAINTED DESCRIPTIONS of nature by an artist in the throes of hypnotic rapture is but the expression of the dualism of being well fed and ideally imaginative. The Grecians with their culture belonged to the well-fed minority, while their slave brethren were more or less inexpressive. So it is that we paint pictures according to our stage of evolution. Well-fedness is the objective stimulus for the nice abstract words or canvas painting. A hungry man has a hungry outlook, and little or no interest in the noctambulist woolgatherings of the nature devotee, who raves away – you know how: A Sky of silken blue, stuccoed with the golden riplets of sunny tints, above hills of green brown majesty. Oh, the muck of metaphor! how you kid the soft high falutin', hungering, shop assistants with such stuff and send them on their Sunday hikes with those back-to-nature rucksacks.

To the hobo the sky is hardly ever noticed, unless it be to see whether it offers mildness or storm; pleasant scenery is totally ignored; only nature in dithyrambic humour is worthy of concern, and only because of its possibility of discomfort. The miles are long and weary; they lead uninterestingly from one town to another.

Man must have some purpose: walking from one town to another is the tramp's.

I remember after a stiff drag, getting to Sheffield – it had been raining since before dinnertime and I got there about seven – I was wet but in clover, possessing a shilling. So I kipped in regal majesty at a place suitably termed 'the six hundred'. (That was its bed capacity.)

What a place! what likeness to God's own image were its inhabitants! Mendicants, navvies, pickpockets, loafers and travellers, all mixed together because of their financial similarity. There once again I heard the spoken word, this time of one section of the people of the abyss. It could be emphatic, it generally was, and even in its humour it was highly coloured and the popular colour was red, and running as though the beat of time, were regular expletives, suggestive of contiguous fecundity.

Try it, you stiff-collared puritans. Get some idea of what men are, outside your little mousetrap circle. Be a human among god's chosen, get contaminated, try your skilled springy rapiers, against their bludgeons; then you will see it is only the benevolence of a caste that permits you to remain like a marionette with trimmed nails and lemon-coloured gloves. Six hundred beds, six hundred occupiers all in varied states of dilapidation, not one matriculated and not one desirous of such an advantage. Each has got down to the tanner-a-bed basis. One scratching, thieving, heterogeneous, merged group, with one common general purpose – the need of a roof, and of a place to sleep. Not one a pauper, not one able to afford anything better; common social financial equality. Brutes and bullies, meek men and softies, fat and thin, some clean, some dirty – just a marine store for the refuse of society. It's a port in a storm for the nomad and the navvy and a haven for the 'local'.

The tramp is away the next morning, he is ever on the move. The day's food and the night's kip is the task to be done. There is no credit, no artificial succour, just plain ingenuity and knowledge of how successfully to beg from a dubious public. One gets the right psychic touch of whom to tap, and whom to leave alone by experience.

Of course in the novitiate stage one makes many mistakes. I wonder if one 'Sky Pilot' remembers my paying him a call. I had read Sheldon's *In His Steps*, and so I thought parsons easy to tap. (Any roadster could have put me wise and proved otherwise.) In earnest I rang the bell and lo! a neat servant answered the door. 'Could I see the Rev'n Gentleman?' My name was sent, and at long last out comes 'His gracious goodness'. 'What could he do?' 'I want a meal,' says I. He put me through a cross-examination which showed the utilitarian value of the experience of the many charity committees he had sat upon. It also proved him more suited to be a lawyer. After tabulating me decent, he sent me to the back of the house where the bitter March wind was blowing fiercely, and out of the back door came more carpets than Brussels ever produced. I was told to shake them. This I did, and eventually was rewarded by a frugal meal of bread and butter, with my fairy godfather looking on with spiritual acidity. Had I been addicted to imbibing the strong waters of men? Was my soul saved? And then to cap it all he opened out, bellowed forth, in the mumming singing monotonics that pass as real reverend godliness and prayed to God for sinners. After this I was shown out and given a message of hope, the hope that God looks after all, both the saints and the sinners. So no more tapping of parsons with their come-to-Jesus sermons and exploitation; two and a half hours' work for one frugal meal!

On I went musing, dreaming, soliloquising, and then constantly coming to earth. How the blinking police had you taped! The cold, professional, steely stare. I remember going to one police station for a putting-up for the night; but they know the law. There is a 'spike' seven miles away, and you are told to 'beat it quick'. Any remonstrance is met with an unceremonious thrust into the middle of the roadway. I found the milk of human kindness improved the more rural I got in location. The John Hodge with his cot and kids seemed incapable of refusing to give a buttered slop-stone to one in need. The hospitality of the village pub was generous. A song and a couple of standard overtures like 'Zampa' or 'William Tell', finished off with the reciting of 'Liberty' by Lord Lytton. This is what they like, and you are right for a pint and a copper collection! They are fine fellows, strong simple souls and kind. How they with their parochialness relished my yarns of worldly town-wisdom, outlines of social science, glitterings of man's development and description of men of great prominence. They never took me to task, even if I did lay it on a little thick; the common ordinariness of a mobile mind was to them the heights of scholarship.

As one nears the metropolis a rapid change of mannerism and human warmth is to be seen. People become 'flyer' and more 'hard-boiled'; they are much less satisfactory. Primmer in dress, yes, more polite and nicer in speech, certainly faster on foot, but always suspicious of your good intent. Their houses are ambitious suburban egg boxes, ornamented by pebbles, and to show their exclusiveness, on each gate one sees 'No hawkers'. Dear Mr Suburban, with your hire-purchase, your endowments (premiums to pay), and your hope of superannuation, how can you live the life of independence? A bungalow, a car, and only one child (of course a superior little angel, not one of the ragamuffin scum), and the desire to get on. Get some spare ribs down you, become healthy, love, live and laugh, fly at mediocre methodism, become hoboes and see the sun. Offend the rota club and the bethel, miss the building society, get off that stodgy office stool, have a good row with your wife's family, get blotto with the booze, have that angel puritan next door collapsing with a stroke and above all things break his windows. Get out of your smug complacency, get action by reaction to your respectable servitude. Look at yourselves, little pigmy satellites, henchmen in offices, travellers for ladies' prayer books, starved, controlled, leashed mongrels. Low stakes for you, ever playing for safety, ever a limit. The sky is the limit to a gambler, but for you, dry feet, one child and a wife that fears poverty. 'Out, out, brief candle', you are not an incandescent.

Even the lobbied houses of the artisans are barren ground, that the seed of your tale and your distress cannot get nutriment from. The two main spots for raking in the 'shove over' are the dense streets of the poorer quarters and the back door of the 'cook's kitchen'. 'Oh Father let thy guilty child, call thee by that sweet name again', 'One word Mother', and 'Lead kindly light' sung to the necessary strength to reach the ears of the impressionable working-class womenfolk, have been the means of pulling many a wayfarer out of the trek to the spike, and setting him, high and dry, in the environs of the 'kip'.

Of course, men can be tapped too, the landlord must be saluted, and then you do your stuff in the tap-room. If there are any Irishmen in, you are landed, for once an Irishman knows a man needs his kip, he is sure to cough up. 'John McAfferee' well sung is sufficient to intimate to your bleary-eyed four-gallon-capacity men your obvious distress. This 'ballad of the ranks' is accepted to be the best of 'musical' compositions, and guaranteed to reach the brain, and register the knock, for the need of alms. The sozzled thickness of grey matter then rids itself a little of its mistiness, and punctures are caused in the morose bag that imprisons melody. Thus the more 'Kayli' the imbiber has had, the more lustily and frantically he roars the chorus, with a special effort to pull himself together, to get out the last lines, 'They made a murderer of Mc-Aff-er-ee.'

The more McAfferee is murdered, the more thirsty they get, and with it the more noisy they become, and Boniface is in a state of confusion between supplying the 'lotion' and wondering 'If the house is being watched'. (Boniface lives by the amount of barrels consumed, his licence is threatened by the 'narrow' notions of Methodists as to right conduct.)

Just as you reach the psychological moment, justifying your going 'round with the cap', most likely some 'assaulter of the earth' (navvy) will jump up, and with a wink from his eye 'Show the man how to sing'. On being eventually made aware of the fact that you have been doing it for 'your bread and cheese', he, despite his thirst for song, subsides with a 'Here's you's are, matey', giving the lead with twopence to your cap. Sometimes you may touch real lucky, two shillings in coppers and a trunk full of 'Lunatic soup'. Out then you stagger, the Goliath of your craft, beating your chest and murmuring with peaceful content,

*'Ye crags and peaks, I am with you once again,*
*I see the eagle soaring o'er the great abyss,*
*I raise my bow, but cannot shoot,*
*'Tis liberty.*
*Blow on, Ye wild winds blow,*
*This is the land of liberty.'*

# Dick Whittington

LONDON, THE HUB OF THE UNIVERSE, the seat of democratic government, Park Lane, Mayfair, Chelsea, Whitechapel and Spitalfields. What a cosmopolitan crew. After months of frogging one makes for the Embankment, where ends the journey of the vagrant – vagrant, the modern tag for the Elizabethan 'Villains' and 'Sturdy Beggars'.

London, the Embankment, the Charing Cross and Waterloo of life's incompatibles. A form every fifty yards. Big Ben at one end and Blackfriars Bridge at the other. The home away from home, the killer of egoism, the gathering of affinities. One-nighters and permanents, newcomers, goers and stoppers. All 'stoney', all on thc lcvel, all can prate about their pasts, few so foolish as to speculate as to their future success.

Out of gaols, out of spike; out of works, out of respects, but all accepting this long promenade's hospitality in preference to that of the one big union – the workhouse. You may have noticed them, they are looked at by the day or week provincial trippers. These sightseers think they are cut-throats and bag snatchers. The mealy-mouthed politician never notices them at all, as he treads his way to 'England's best club', the house of gas. Poverty is with us eternally, there is companionship in numbers, relief of mind is given by seeing many in a worse plight than yourself. Get down to the dregs and you stay there. What chance has any of these-my-sisters on Piccadilly, with its lights showing their lines of premature haggardness, their poverty, their pinchedness? No man has for a bedmate a siege-stricken moll. Yes, they're in siege, rarely relieved. The heavens cry out for vengeance.

Oh London of Dick Whittington, you are infested with people of poverty, your crypts under St Martin's in the Fields, your bridges, your night-shelters, your Starvation Army. Where else can you place them? There are ever so many more, all needing your motherly breast.

And in the centre of gravity, we are making world history, bringing to England the Glory that is hers, hanging the Kaiser. Oh my dear orator how you kidded us. Your straight from the shoulder earnestness that I fell for is now resting so peacefully on some snow-white feather bed.

What interest have we in your pageantry, your changing of the Guard, your Wembleys, Tussauds and Unknown Warrior's Grave. They only appeal to the trippers and the yapping horn-rimmed 'Yanks'. Just as they flit from this sight to that in the day, we at night shuffle to catch an odd rescue van here and there, with its benevolent cup of tea.

Have you seen the crown jewels at the Tower? Have you seen the queue at midnight at Trafalgar Square patiently waiting for their free drink of tea? Have you been to the Aldwych, to hear Tom Walls in his farcical witticisms? Have you been interrogated by the policeman before he gives you a button entitling you to sit in the cellar of a church until morning? Have you heard the Kit-Cat band playing 'Goodnight, beloved'? Have you heard Big Ben strike with its droning vibrating mellow tone in the stark chilly eerie hours of the morning?

Having tasted this civilised vintage of wineless chill, I decided sensibly to make my getaway and once again turn to the green fields and pastures new. It's a good day's drag to get beyond the city's environs. Northernwards now becomes the trek, slowly drifting through, through time; here and there getting a bed, sometimes creeping into a barn, sometimes under a hedge.

Cambridge is reached. There are the future men of greatness, the silver spooners, mostly of good physique, some scorching the roads like mad demons, some having an air of stupendous study, mostly having a sangfroid and bantering clownishness; all having that hallmark of born superiority, a cross between arrogance, importance, and complete at-ease-ment. Dovetailed here and there between these standard potential pure English plutocrats, giving a glimpse of the world commonwealth of money's privilege is a Jap, a Froggie, a sallow-looking product of India, a darkey from Africa – all going through the pacings to fit them to make their way as the Caesars, Popes, Bankers, Judges, Bishops, Politicians, and so on down to the humble doctors, the men of literature, the men of architecture – privileged supervisors of the proletarian army of fustians. I looked at their colleges. They were too ancient to impress, only their traditions, their caste purity, their confidence of immutableness keeps them put.

The things I noticed most were the number of second-hand clothing dealers, the dumped books of knowledge, all the resurrections from the no longer needed sections of embryo importancies – wardrobes and desks. Having the English characteristic of a gambler, I decided while being so near, to see Newmarket, the headquarters of the gees that had carried my money in times of frugal affluence. In this town of men of small stature my five feet seven seemed like a giant's. What a nice little chapel the King then had for his stable boys. Middle-aged Harry Marsh, fat and of the old roast-beef type, came bowling down the drive in a trap similar to what I had seen on trotting courses. I have only the native's replies to my questions as to which place was which and which notability was this or that. Harry Lines was king of the selling-platers then; R. Day had a big string, stayers were his specialities and he was fairly successful. Noticing the gallops on the heath, I was struck with the straightness of the course the horses took, they never seemed to zigzag – what a perfection in training. The turf worn deep by constant galloping was straight and even, as though someone had mown strips of length alternately. Days came and went, with a sixty seconds to the minute velocity. I, a bird of passage, kept on plodding along.

# Sleep

THE SPIKE, A NAME HAVING THE TOUCH of the romantic, the substitute for the long-past almshouses – where the good old monks used to welcome the weary, lame and lazy, welcome them with the cheer of nut-brown beer and bread and cheese; in the morning give them a parting blessing, 'In the name of the Father and of the Son and of the Holy Ghost' – Elizabeth, with your protestantism, you changed all that. National glories like Pembroke, Raleigh and Grenville were in the van of robbery and of rent squeezing. You had 'ten thousand vagabonds infesting the roads, begging and stealing', many of whom had been divorced from the land by enclosure acts. At Middlesex Sessions in 1575, forty-four vagabonds were sentenced to be branded, five to be hanged, and eight set to service. Service was unvarnished slavery. And it was from the stress of such times that humanity set up its workhouses; we still have them with us.

Over three hundred years of civilised evolution, and still

the workhouse for the native, and the spike for the rover, the propertyless are still with us, they are multiplied over a hundred times. England prides itself about such institutions, the spike, the vagrancy ward, the only place left to a constitutionalist who happens to be flattened out. You get there about 5.30 and find others there like yourself, waiting aimlessly and fatigued, spread along the road, making a picture of untidiness to the eye of the aesthetic. Slowly a distant thin chained army is streaming in dribbles to the bottom of this road, the prelude, the wait, for the opening of the spike. Their standard bundle is first a canvas (sacking) bag or wrapping and a brewing-up tin. The bag contains dockers (cigarette stumps), humorously termed 'pavement mixture', a brewing or two (tea and sugar), an odd nail or two, one or two intimates' photos, discharge papers, relics of former sweetness, and a plentiful supply of toe-rags, plus string, paper and soap. The feet are the tramp's great concern, they are his main-spring: if they get knocked up, he is out of the business, so it is that he looks well after them according to the habits of his fraternity; toe-rags, soap and papers are the dressing of first aid.

You squat down, just nod and wait events. Eventually someone from amongst you languidly asks where you are from, and where you are going next; you swop hints and advice. After a bit one of the group gets up and walks to the entrance gateway for casuals. Slowly and reluctantly everyone else follows. The porter takes your kit, name, and nationality, where from, where to, and you shuffle to a receiving room. To this comes an attendant, he gives you a can of tea and a slice of rooty (bread and marge). He takes you maybe four at a time to some stone sinks. There you drop your clothes, bundle them to be taken away, stand in the sink, and catch the lump of carbolic he without ceremony throws. Water comes from a poor kind of shower over your head and you proceed to bathe yourself. Then you are thrown a long shirt, two blankets, and you proceed for the night to a generally bedless chamber. Next morning you are up, washed, given back your clothes: they are all creases, and sometimes fumigated. You line up, the taskmaster looks you over and back you go to the receiving room where bread marge and tea is consumed again. An attendant comes with the layout, some get a free exit (only a few, who have convinced the taskmaster they are on the way to a job). The rest get good honest labour, from stonebreaking to woodchopping.

I remember my first experience. 'I'll finish these four stones in ten minutes,' says I. Bump, bump, bump, went the hammer. By good hefty hitting they were broken up in about thirty minutes. I punched at the door of the cell I was in. After a while the taskmaster came wanting to know 'What the B—— H——'s up.' I told him I had done the job and wanted to be on my way. 'Look here, son, you have got to put what you break through that grating, all of it, and you must leave your cell spotless.' When I examined what he called the grating, it was an opening the size of a yard square, placed four feet up. It had bars across and these prevented anything too big being thrown through. The stones I had vigorously knocked stuffings out of were still much too large. Bump, bang, bump, more bang, bump, bimp: it took three hours' hard pelting to get through the task. Of course the value of your work is little or nothing, but it is a deterrent against making spikes places of paradise.* No man need go destitute. If you roam about at night without visible means of support you are placed in quod. The casual ward is the puritans' safety valve. The best of them are only ports in a storm and the vast majority nauseating to the independent wish that is placed in man's soul. Heavens save us from promoted paupers (a section of regular inmates, who by their trustworthiness are placed in positions of trust and semi-boss-ship; they generally

* Everyone did not get stonebreaking, only the more robust. Coming down the road later with an old tramp, he said things had greatly improved. Prior to 1900 a fixed task was imposed of 18 cwt of stones or 4 lb of oakum. (You then worked until task was completed, no matter how long it took; often well into darkness by candlelight.) Afterwards 'conscientious effort of a reasonable time' was accepted. I don't think there is much, if any, stonebreaking done now. Woodchopping and various fatigues associated with the Union seem to obtain. The Ministry of Health insists today on a bath, one warm meal and a bed. Still, now you don't get the same chance of a quick getaway. You are kept in a full day: say from Tuesday 5 p.m. to Thursday 7.30 a.m. There are no releases on Sundays.

get for payment, sugar in their tea), from martinet taskmasters. I often laugh (ironically) at reports of boards of Guardians' meetings (now called P.A.C.) with their glib suggestion of luxuries for their casuals.

Pough! These tender-hearted rate-savers doing well for society's luckless! Between their piety and 'liberal' economy even Gandhi would become a bolshie. Good men and women, all giving their time and energy to make the hobo comfortable! They work on the principle of trying to drive him away. Each little shopkeeper public-minded skinflint thinks it is fair game, fair game to make their casual ward less enticing than their next nearest. If this can be done, they say, our friends on the 'George Robey' will give our place a miss and we will be freed from the financial burden. And pray, what consideration should these roving harum-scarums have? Don't they refuse to be decent human beings? Why don't they settle down, go to Sunday School and work for sixpence an hour? Yes, my dear friend, if you go to Sunday School, work hard, accept meekly the humble 'under the trade union rate', you can be Barnum's biggest bums but, character (sterling thing) will dub you 'Honest, willing, sober and safe'.

Of my trek back to Lancashire is little more that need be said; perhaps you will take it for granted – spikes, kips, and roughing it (roughing it means sleeping out). Still you might suffer a little longer, while I describe the kip houses. Try three or four of them, and notice the difference (the price for the night varies from sixpence to a shilling).

Sample the Salvation Army ones. They are practically all alike, just like the Maypole or Woolworth, wherever there's a town there's a 'Sall Doss'. The same direction seems to be over all of them. You have to submit to a routine. If you want anything you must get it from them. They provide no fires – the places are heated otherwise. So you cannot get the old frying pan crackling; the sizzle of onions and spare ribs is never to be at Salvation Army hostels. They provide, for payment, all food and tea.

Mostly casuals prefer to go elsewhere if it is convenient. On Sundays, or some slack night during the week, some of their gallant lassies might come; and the room takes on the atmosphere of wrestling with the torments of the soul. There's the usual healthy devoutness about the 'Hallelujahs' and 'Praise be the Lord's'. It may be all right. But I found myself reluctant to stay there with such Christian virginity. It is much used by the steadier and also appeals to the mooching, job-begging type. Its general characteristics are: cleanliness, institutionalism, and just a suspicion that you are being blest by God's soldiers, even though you pay the Devil's money.

If you can swallow being rescued, hymned and prayed for, buying weak tea, the Salvation Army sell tickets out at reduced rates.

Now for the average type of common lodging house. Their faults are: they are not too clean, have too many in a bedroom, many of the regulars are too noisy in their booze and the deputy is generally a poor weak crater who wants bribing for any little service he renders. The advantages are: a big warm fire of coke and coal (maybe two), plenty of pans, mugs, and tables, open access to them – you can cook at any time you like anything you have. During times of briskness – say, a big reservoir is being made – there is often a greater influx of travellers who come to sleep. It is then – if the local authorities are not extremely vigilant – that what is termed 'a sit up' obtains. This means you are permitted to sit in a chair and charged about half the price of a bed. Of course there's a fire, but generally no light. Yes, my dears, early to bed and early to rise. A sit up is a grand thing if you have the price of it. I have seen as many as twenty pay for the privilege.

Now for the palaces of kip-dom, the corporation (municipal) models, and the Rowtons. They are the Rolls-Royces. Them are the blue ribbands (them is). Price: about one shilling a night. Attendants, sometimes in uniforms, baths, tailors and cobblers' shops, each of which specialise in cheap touch-ups; a system, a routine, and, I believe, a profit. Now, Mr Town Councillor, get one in your town. If you have one, get another for they are always full, there are always more turned away than can get in. Give the homeless a place fit to be in and worth staying at. If you make profits, well; though I abhor them, in this case you will be welcome.

Back to sanity, settled once again in my old sleepy little industrial town, just a little more wild, a little less pleased with citizenship. Everything seems as it was. The parsons are preaching, the masters are being toadied and respected, the working men are hustling and scamping their work, the corner boys are looking for cheap drinks, and the feminine outdoor workers seem to be flourishing as much as ever, such is my impression of my return to the town of my birth.

# Beastly Blondes

MOST OF MY MATES HAVE uneventfully fallen into the way of working for their living. Most of them greet me and seem proud of their lot. They think they can perform the functions of this favourite recreation of the working class, better than their fellows. 'I can eat the b—— job', is a common expression. Beastly blondes of toil, willing, eager, eaters up of production. To me they are overdoing it. I think they work too hard and think too little. But they know they are good ones at it, and work never killed anyone, not hard work. Even working men do at times die. The stimulus to existence is work, it is life's sole purpose. Work for a decent wage if possible, but work certainly. For regularity and plenty of it hard, many are prepared to do it under the odds. Of course they thought the work game would go on for ever. Rationalisation has now made their services less important, thank goodness. Poor cattle, full of pomposity when adorned in a new suit off Montague Burton's. Tailor made! What tailor could meet their slender purses and yet hide the fact that they are toilers? Where is their poise, straightness, carriage, where is their elasticity of heel; what collar could rest unwrinkled when their bony collarbones stick out so generously? How can one's head sit graciously, when the nape of the vertebrae aches with jaded exhaustion? Such is the price of eating the b—— job. What mental recreation is acceptable to the fatigued body? None, only the artificial manufactured kind. Horseology, cardology, beerology, and sexology.

Man is the creature of conditions – environment; if the brute is overworked he generally cannot think. That must be done for him by Edgar Wallace, Winalot, and the Bow St Reporter. Of course this is for the good. What is nicer than hewing wood and drawing water to the thoughts of 'What's going to win the Two-Thirty?' or 'Yes, he has to hang by the neck until dead.' Possible fortune on one hand and glorious better-than-he on the other.

Somehow or other I drifted back into 'this return to work' craze. With it came consequent decay. As some would say 'It's an ignorant way of getting a living; the many think it to be divine.' Fridays: see the eagle excrete its golden eggs (wage envelope) and so you feel that there is something in it after all; but when Monday comes 'I have my doubts.' Believe me there is quite a knack in this work game. It calls for a strategy of its own. One must not speak in working hours; neither must one smoke (whistling or humming a hymn might be permitted). Take the first day of my return. Like a mug, I set about it. 'Get it done' says I, and have a limerick (rest) afterwards. It is like physic – take a big swig and get it over. I was wise, I was. Eight o'clock, stuck into it, by eleven, something attempted, something done, I've earned the right to a brief repose. That's being conscientious and sensible, that is. But there's a foreman and over him a manager. They don't like you having a blow. They look black at you, talk about packs of cards being in the office and having your money ready. So rather than be dubbed no good, you get into it again and defer your limerick until you get home.

This makes you wiser than you thought you were. You alter your tactics, as a runner changes his speed from a sprint to a mile. Still, by the system of foremen and managers they push you on faster than humans should travel. I have often wondered which firm will introduce roller skates first, Henry Ford's I suppose. I find out my idea of a good man is wrong. I thought craftsmanship was admirable. The firms however wanted good, fast and cheap workers, with speed and cheapness the essentials. We industrially lived in an age of make-believe. The manager hustled the production of spurious product, the foreman was an understrapper, and the men, well, just BEASTLY BLONDES.

Have you not yet seen through Understrapper, Mr Reader? Understrapper, the boot-licking foreman: the proud pet of his satellite cronies, who lush him with free beer. Never absent, never late, crawling, creeping, ever answering 'His Master's Voice' or whim. What the boss says 'goes', except when understrapper ham bones (pinches) half the works to make a blanket box. Between the boss and the missus, the foreman's life is full of bliss. What a heart of gold he possesses. He glories in firing better blokes than he, because they are men. By sucking, stealth and fear of displacement, he has risen a halfpenny an hour higher than his men, with first preference for overtime. His cronies laugh at his rare barren jokes, fall in with his idolatrous belief in the sun shining through the boss's posterior; strikes are sacrilege and anathema; harmony, goodwill and leaving it to the boss is the one sure way to prosperity. Of course, they know different; it is but camouflage to cover up their half-bakedness. Understrappers are the drones of the working class, the inefficients, the redundants, the most easily displaceables. I know you do not agree with me, Mr Employer. That is your funeral, many have been on your payroll for years by their crying, sneaking, lying and pandering to your pompous vanity. What are the dynamics of this work thrust? First: it is a necessary evil, the only means left to the proletariat of capturing the loaf. Secondly, it happens to be an accustomed habit of an orthodox majority and it is aided by the inherent slave instincts of an unfortunate ancestry (Pyramids, Roman Galleys, Tied Cotter, nineteenth-century factory worker) and thirdly, there happens to be a faint hope in the prospects of promotion (understrapping).

The ambitious group of climbers fall willingly for all the nauseating repugnant tricks that help to category them as suitable products for the stripes (promotion). What are these tricks? Sneaking is quite a common one! Working like blazes when flannel foot, the manager, silently creeps around, is another; getting others to commit indiscretions is also a good winning number, such as: 'I wouldn't b—— well do that', and getting a mug to make a stand on the point, so putting him in the soup. Oh yes; the won't-do-its will do anything, it's just a trap for the innocents. Going to the pub, club or bethel of the firm's heads is another trump card, whining tales about little children and ailing wives are sometimes resorted to. Splitting on, or magnifying any little thing that some exploited worker ventilates.

These are done for what? Work, being kept on and a meagre wage each week. 'Ambition should be made of sterner stuff.' 'There is more in *life* than is dreamt of in your philosophy, Horatio'; and says Caesar, 'Let me have men about me that are fat; sleek-headed men, and such as sleep o' nights: Yon Cassius has a lean and hungry look; he thinks too much: such men are dangerous.' Few victimised workers could get support from mates employed with him. No factory inspector could get a wise employee to complain about time cribbing, dangerous conditions or rates below the Board of Trade scale. Seldom do these hardy sons of toil muff. Whistle, start, stop, day in and day out, always trying to give satisfaction and be kept on is the will of the class.

Life's continuity? It ends at your death: till then I must survive; I'll win through, I'll do anything; they must keep me on, the hurly burly, the rough and tumble, the humdrum continuity. Still, dear work animal, your main crime is self-denial and individual cut-throatism. From wailing Egyptian slave and Roman captive down to Henry Ford's model robots, the blessings bestowed to the earth can be seen by all; all that is or will be stands as objective monuments to the utilitarianism and productivity of these despicable slaves, the John Hodges, the Henry Dubbs and those vulgarly termed the uncouth men in fustians.

So time passes on; sometimes I am working, sometimes unemployed, then looking for a fresh job. Life drags on. It may seem idiotic to tell you that I have been fired again for talking whilst at work. Such is the freedom won by the long evolutionary march to 'Eldorado'. What an anachronism to be caught exercising your even limited vocabulary. Exuberance, verbosity, they are the private preserves of the politicians and the reverend gentlemen. What a crime to speak! Visions of Forums, Antony's Orations, Lawyers Quips! Anyway why bother about being sacked? Work is a plague; it's ugly; still it's part of us. How empty is our life without it. We are desirous of returning to it. It is our life's purpose.

# Affinities

CUPID WITH HIS ARROWS, the little creation of the mind, the little mischievous disturbing boy, the one who refuses to take 'No' for an answer, the little god that laughs, laughs and conquers.

It is, I am afraid, an indiscriminate cupid that hangs around the parading grounds from which the hitching of most working-class couples emanates. He just lets fly about two hundred arrows in an ordinary street, and there's Bills, Joes and Jacks saying 'How do' to the Marys, Mays and Lizzies. Then there is a chase or crawl according to the confidence of the parties, another 'How do', a stop and the usual question, 'Aren't you going for a walk?' – Ain't love grand – so Romantic. . . . If the little minx you pull up happens to live in a parloured house, etiquette demands that she says, 'No; not tonight', but she lets you know she must gradually become more familiar. How Victorian. If she lives in a one up and one downer, well, she weighs you up to see whether you're what she terms 'a mess'. If her scrutiny passes you O.K. she blurts: 'I don't mind, where are we going, in't chip 'oil?' (Chip 'oil, otherwise chip shop, is the Lancashire working-class Trocadero.)

Romance, what a rapturous beginning for the sex urge to get on its milky way. There are streets for learners, streets for those who have passed through, and streets for the 'posh' folk, and in each and every street there is 'Bobby-move-them-on', giving assurance to the old women's sewing class as to the good morality of the town.

It seems just a miscarriage of justice, which lass marries which lad, but it so happens, the consolation is, if you did not marry this girl, you most likely would have married that.

You decide as to the goodness of your choice later, by comparing your beloved to someone else's who is not as good (in your opinion), and you decide as to your misfortune by comparing her to somebody else who has turned out better (again in your opinion). It is all a matter of relativity. Good fortune, opportunity, and things running smooth makes for better husbands and better wives. Bad luck, constantly struggling against adversity makes for misconceptions, charges of dragging your mother-in-law's daughter down, and so on.

Courtships can last quite a long while if your mother puts her foot down. She looks upon the girl as trying to steal her innocent child. She knows, for she stole dad; besides, she is not too well blessed and needs you to take your wages home a little longer.

Most of the girls know little or nothing about sex matters, other than what they have learned in that educative circle known as the card or ring room.* They take, if it happens, their misfortune with stoic complacency and after the news getting circulated seem nonchalant.

There is no undue sloppiness about 'getting off' or 'knocking on' as it is called. Judging by the numerosity of the love birds anyone will do. Of course there is a bit of something to recommend about the pairing, it is that, the more one gets to know another, the more magnified becomes the beauty and the special distinct qualities of your favoured one.

Prospects seem to count very little: just a little wisecrack, a smiling countenance, or a spritely ankle, makes a tart fit for continued attention, and a good bit of devil-may-careness, or in its absence a free application of lard on the hair, does the trick for the proletarian sheik.

So the age-long suicide approaches. Saleeby is not consulted, blood tests are things unknown. Nature does its business and blind chance decides the answer.

Thcrc is many a tiff, some get chucked up, sometimes there is chopping and changing, but behind it all, there is just nature in the raw.

* Rooms where preparations of cotton spinning take place.

The Queen Bee at times becomes alluring, gets given to buying hair slides and nick nacks, even resorting to permanent waves of temporary life, via the club (a shilling a week) method.

The rough-spun HE MAN, modulates his voice, sometimes cleans his teeth, waits hours in the rain: them's the symptoms of love, them is. It is as old as the hills and as inescapable as St Helena. What a beast I was, I loved 'em, and clouted 'em, picked and chucked (among the seconds, of course), until at last I saw the inevitability of marriage; it was an institution. I saw it only too clearly. I strove bravely, indefatigably and ferociously to dim its obviousness – how like a man. I wanted to escape it, but alas, orthodoxy, thou always wins. I knew it possessed no single advantage, either for lass or lad. It was imprisonment, and personality-destroying. It was poverty-producing and the creator of servitude. The trouble would be little ones. It meant being reconciled to being a work-animal, a flag-waving supporter of keep-your-job-ism. It was a life of responsibility. Ownership with commitments, owning a woman, with legal responsibilities. Desertion would make one liable for half your earnings, one would have to stick it or have a quid a week worked off him. Owning a few sticks called furniture, four years of your future pledged to so much per week. The club man, the rent man, the butcher, the baker, the candlestick maker, all knocking expectantly at the door. Love in a cottage, how blissful and sweet, pay all your debts before you can eat.

Despite this obvious recognition of marriage's disabilities, the bally thing took place. With it came, not the entrancing mysteries of the bedroom, nor the passionate soul-stirring emotion of two sugar-candied Darby and Joans, but the practical resolves, that come what may, be the furnisher's dues met or no, the rent paid or spent, we – the wife and I – would commemorate our marriage by having, on every Sunday morn, ham and eggs for breakfast. So it was we got one over on the poet with his madness of love, the little dove birds, etc.

From marriage came the settling down, the period of consolidation – settling in the real sense, settling of bills associated with hire purchase in particular; settling in the general, with the wife becoming a poor cheese-paring domestic drudge, and poor hubby, breaking himself in to limited pence, regular hours, and tame moderation in habits, almost on a par with a blue-eyed-Saxon-regular-Sunday-School-good-lad. Still we always had Sunday's breakfast to look forward to.

Marriage, monogamy, one man, one woman, until death doth us part. Marriage, to some a sacrament, a thing sacred; to others, just a compliance with custom, a formality. Some marry because they are afraid to test if their mutual appeal is strong enough to keep them together, they must have some compelling force. One man, one woman. Does it work out that way? Divorces galore! Even some of the working classes are having them now. Poor men's still cost about twenty pounds. If they come down to seven and sixpence, well it would test the success or failure of marriage. One man, one woman. The constancy of the wife, the constancy of the husband!

I think nearly all wives are constant to their partners: yes, until the end of the marriage. Is this true of the male? I doubt it. Poor man, he tries his best, he does try, but somehow like the pledge he signs, he is sure to break out. Most men will deny it, you in your righteous indignation may stone me; but man thou are not true. Man, the superior creature to woman! This is, I think, physiological and not through man's frailness. I feel sure that the magnificent struggles they put up to avoid the occasional fall are worthy of them, but somehow the strength to struggle successfully is not sufficient. What do you think about that, Mr Monogamist? Are you still going to continue with your cant and denials. Of course all little boys are spanked for telling a fib, they become red in the face when caught. A man is a little boy in these things; he denies, until he realises it is silently accepted that such things are, but they must never be admitted.

Constancy in civilised England is woman's sole expression. Men do try to be so also, they keep on trying: most of them are constant in their trying.

Man in his greatness oft gets down to the animal when the sun sets and darkness appears. He knows it is a mug's game. He would, if not good mannered, smack any dame in the mouth after drinking at her magic fount. After he has reflected, admonished himself for his weakness, filled himself with fears of infection, he slowly resolves to overcome this libertine fecundity, be able to face the eyes of his sweet-tempered, constant, domesticated appendage at home by being constant and true.

This he does for a time, but mind being subjected to matter, the matter of legs, skirts and rouge, conquers the mind of parochial intent. He knows that the only absolute preventative in the promiscuous stakes is the inability to draw breath.

Still, he is not to blame, the lure and the call of the wild are things deep down in his primitive soul; they are part of his subconscious self, his normality is being a tender loving husband, but acting under aphrodisiac surroundings of sirens, scent, cosmetics and rustling skirts, that dormant polygamous instinct of his primitive father reasserts itself. Really, though some men are less afflicted than others, I do not think it is a moral question; it is purely physical; possibly the day may come, when some hard-boiled corrector will give us a prescription to overcome such sickness.

Having studied men, I find they are ever open to accept fleeting moments of indiscretions, in fact many make it their principal hobby. Those who affect to be satisfied with monogamy, possessing wives that are good, kind and true, are men that would play up ructions, brand and castigate, look with eyes of enraged treachery, consider the bed of sanctity corrupted, putrified, fouled, and rotted, if their wife was even platonic with some Adonis.

They are men who would kill, men who would defend themselves by the unwritten law, talk about the right of revenge, do 'Othello' on the bare suspicion of a wife's folly. 'Each man kills the thing he loves,' says Oscar Wilde.

Possession is the right of man and does not include any form of sharing.

Women of Lancashire, you are finer than men; even more philanthropic than they. You feed the brute of a husband, you continue your life of mill industry; you drudge and table the beefsteak, you recognise his mastership, amid it all you are proud of him, and devote much of your muchness to keeping him with you till the end of your tether.

Marriages continue to take place, the breakfasts get eaten, the photographers get a job, the parsons beam, the women in the snug get their shilling, scandals are rampant, suggestions of 'just in time' are whispered aloud, there's announcements in the papers and so on. The evenness of wedding performances passes and passes; each has his or her day, seeing that it is an event of events in two poor souls' lives. 'Here is health, wealth and happiness', and may they all make whoopee.

After this inescapable foolishness, I became a little John Wesley (pardon the term), a nipper, a squeezer, a scraper, a saver, fixed with the fixedness of getting on. I took an interest in the many ramifications of husbandry, considered endowments (this was pushed upon me by a pelmanised superintendent of an insurance club). I viewed it at first with the eagerness of an optimist who is confident of success; after much weighing up, I faltered, got pessimistic, and by abuse, cunning and stubbornness warned off the insurance company's virile servant, so breathing freely with the knowledge of two and sixpence a week less to find for the next fifty years of a problematical future. The same happened as a conclusion of the study of the vagaries of Building Societies. The owners by instalment, I saw, had a skeleton in each cupboard of each proudly possessed bungalow. It was quarter day; and a twenty years blackmail before the ghost would subside. This I am pleased I escaped from.

I became a modern economist, a practical socialist. No financiers, or companies – be it the attraction of annuities for the last portion of my life or a bungalow of my own after twenty years of quarterly tributes – would drain me to the dregs. Damn them and their extortions. I would live in a hovel, enjoy the advantage of my landlord being parliamentarily kept under by rent restriction acts, and to show my rebellion occasionally, I would give even him a miss. I would invest all my hitherto wasted surpluses in sixpenny stamps, buy savings certificates – five shillings a week for ten years makes so much, plus something for nothing interest, and if things turn out bad the advantage of withdrawal without losing a penny.

So life became rose-coloured, back in a job, a weekly

screw, a wife of the type that makes no trouble; all that was required was tenacity, Saxon grit, fair fortune and on with the show.

So it was with many of us. Thrift, diligence, enterprise, and initiative, would reward us with happiness, success, and maybe an autumn's retirement leaning over the garden wall, chatting with the retired superannuated police sergeant.

Strong hands would be always needed by the boss, even if he was possessed of that 'lean and hungry look'. Youth could give him his pound of flesh, care and economy could build up a nest egg that would lead to independence of him. Ambition was the thing that would stimulate personal promotion. Silas-Hockingism returned to me again; the righteous, the frugal, the noble, the sober, willing and deserving, would eventually come out on top. The will-to-do was the thing.

I would work and save; hard work would kill no man; it was a certain way, a safe, sure, gradual way, of week by week putting by the old five shillings. Sometimes it would be difficult; then there must be extra-special skinflintism, even walking to and from work, on wet as well as fine days. I would do without that morning swallow of smoke, at night I would talk to the old-age pensioner next door, play ludo and tiddlywinks: anything to perform the feat of putting away for the rainy day. Old bonny face* would be sacked permanently. Only Sundays would be exempt from this

* The Publican.

determined effort to follow the path of the self-made man, from kerbstone to castle. Sunday must be a day of gorging, ham and eggs in boco, the usual half a cow for dinner and currant bread for tea; then a walk around, with pipe filled, puffing away contentedly; something attempted, something done, another five shillings in the post office and the gladdening warmth of more to follow.

[illegible]
[illegible] the [illegible]
[illegible]
[illegible]
[illegible]
[illegible]

# The Great Unwashed

I HAD HOPED TO SUCCEED by steadily saving. Unfortunately periods of unemployment came along and, alas, like many, my humpty dumpty fell off the wall before it had been built a few courses high, and for several years I adopted a process of climbing and falling, until at last I knew the days of paradise, the days of the permanence of work, had finished. Each year would give me less, sooner or later I would be on the scrapheap with the ever-increasing number of redundants, the permanents, 'the won't works', 'the great unwashed'.

Gradually it came about, less work, more unemployment. The bank goes no matter how careful you are, or how economic the wife is with your wages plus dole (period of part-time employment); this under-employment makes you short and with tears in eyes, regrets in your hearts, the thing happens, you draw on your savings. The savings that have nowhere near reached the amount for retirement. There it goes, save and scrape, tenacity, diligence, and trying, what does it amount to? You finish up like the rest – the spenders of our class, the prolific breeders, those anti-Eugenists, the indifferent and the hopeless, who have nothing to meet the rainy day and so are forced to rush up to the Public Assistance Committee for an umbrella. The umbrella of relief. The far-seeing worker has provided himself with his own umbrella, but no matter how stout it is, no matter how strong, the wind blows, the rain rains, the storm gets worse and worse, it becomes a drift, a blizzard, a tornado and at some point or other his umbrella is useless. Its cloth becomes worn and holey and he by the evolutionary levelling-down process has to become totally dependent on the benevolent magnitude of social legislation. I have, due to my unemployment, watched very closely how these unemployment benefit acts have worked. The main thing that all have recognised is – that the scheme is one of insurance – that to me has been its fundamental failing. No scheme can become a commercial success that deals with such a large minority of permanent unemployed. The men certainly need benefits, ethics, humanity; and justice demands they should have them, but it is not possible on the basis of stamp contribution.

That has been the impossible task of the various governments, each trying to make the sums collected balance what has had to be paid out. They have tried all sorts of dodges, the principal one has been going into debt and intending to pay it off when each year dawned with its trade revival – what hopes! Still, they have paid out more than any prudential would dream of doing, their insurance policy is in a state of bankruptcy; but the ordinary man in the street believes it is hush money, money to keep the unemployed from Bolshevism, money paid out to ease the difficult times that the former 'beastly blondes' are meeting so finely. I have no complaint with it; only be honest, face the facts, recognise man's right to work or maintenance. You, my dear politician, have never done that, you stick to the principle of payment on the basis of contributions, the desire is ever with you to make it practical but you always recognise with true statesmanship that the quality of the unemployed changes with the quantity. The more unemployed there are, then the less should the fund be able to stand the strain of benefits – that's logic – but the more unemployed there are, the more urgent becomes the need for you to forget insurance, you are compelled reluctantly to *give*. You must keep up the equilibrium of constitutionalism and the price is – feed the lambs and the hungry multitude with bread – feed them, never forget that, or the biological law of nature, the law of a species' determination to continue in existence, is threatened – and then along comes the modern Antony crying to the multitudes: 'Mischief thou art afoot; do thy stuff.'

You give an unemployed man no sympathy for being unemployed. It is the aggregation of great bulks of unemployed that raises up the cry for labour exchanges, and the setting up of relief schemes. Yes, such circumstances even push the parsons and the salvation armies to open up soup kitchens and dole out second-hand trousers.

The problem of how to deal with this question has been the poison that has killed every government, one after the other, each has been sacked for the failure to solve it. Labour has been charged with offering doles instead of work by the tories, and the unemployed have on the other hand damned them for their meanness in not giving sufficient.

Their vague stand for work or adequate maintenance has really been of a purely liberal cheap cheese-paring type. The tories have looked upon the dole as an unfortunate but necessary evil, but one that must on no account be a means of countering the financial advantages of work. They say: we will pay you to keep you quiet, but like poor-law relief it must be on the minimum basis acceptable. They therefore indulge in the many little, but economical, dodges that the technicians are so clever at. They prune the scales, wipe off sections – sections are not dangerous to the tory equilibrium – sometimes it is the 'gap', sometimes stamps qualifications are overhauled, clauses are deliberately inserted to strike sections off benefits. These are camouflaged by the pretence of preventing sponging.

You with your tory psychology think they prefer to loaf about on a sum I've known many of you pay for a cigar. Yes, Henry, there are brands of cigars that politicians smoke that cost over fifteen shillings each. One advantage of the instability of governments has been their shortness of life and the slowness of the cumbersome parliamentary machine, even for reaction.

Each government has commenced a programme for the remodelling of the acts, each generally as a prelude to their operations temporarily restore men to benefits and then fortunately before the real adverse effects (to the unemployed) could be operated in toto, a political crisis has come, the government gets shipwrecked and the man in the street, with his desire for a change, sends a fresh crew with an equally faulty compass to plough through the turbulent seas of modern capitalistic world chaos.

The new men in the basket of parliament's balloon take up most of their time floundering at the mercy of the winds of disorder, which is associated with the breakdown of the times; eventually their gas is exhausted and lo! there is another ignoble descent. The only way out of the paradox of overproduction is restoring to the vast consuming populations of the world, the benefits of their creative genius. Man must be related to society's productivity, economy is senseless amid plenty, doing without is daft when the cupboard is full. Work or full maintenance is the practical solution to society's ills. The created surplus of the present, with the troubles it is causing, is but the counterpart of the directive policy of making men starve (if starving is too strong a term, let us say stinting). Every political party has ladled out buckets of sympathy, this is akin to Falstaff's conception of honour. It neither heals, fills nor feeds. Just imagine the political Iago, with his sheaf of papers and stance like a Blackpool pill-seller, his qualified utterances that would do justice to a crab moving backwards. He is as straight as a corkscrew and becomes a sleight-of-hand illusionist on the stage of talkology.

'I stand,' says he, sitting in the chair of sympathy, 'in this time of trial, desirous of improving the lot of our unfortunate brothers in the industrial storm of the economic blizzard. I hope to see sometime in the future the return of the Indian summer of prosperity. I feel somehow that that time is not far distant. It may even be upon us now, still if not now, certainly as soon as you return men like me to parliament: men with broad vision, warm hearts and considerate temperaments. Men filled with the milk of human kindness, men who will go there determined to stand (sitting) on the floor of the house, for a bettering of the rough and tumble of life's hurly burly.

'What is wanted is mutual tolerance, a recognition of that sterling character of the British nation, of the nobleness of the men of the county of Lancashire, of the grit, the fortitude and the citizenship of this town of ours. Our town with its shades of progressive policy which holds dearly the memories of —— (insert here some man warm in their hearts). We want the coordination of all our people's combined qualities to make for a conquering of this terrible scourge, that is rampant throughout the world today.

'Have we not had our misfortunes before, our hungry

forties, our cotton panics? Did we not bear them, and did not things get eventually better? Much better; in fact we found ourselves better off than ever before, the richer and the mightier than ever, and the more contented. Let no man get jaundiced by his desponding discomfort – a thing painful but temporary. It may be just a cloud, a temporary cloud; it is a long lane has no turning; we must be near the ford, we are near the end. I feel sure, in fact if you only knew what I have confidentially been put in possession of, you would see that England and its inhabitants could look forward to coming out of this world phenomenon more advantageously than any other country, like a lion refreshed standing supremely the king of the beasts – excuse me, I mean – the leaders of world progress. You may think you have been treated unfairly, still times have been bad, you must remember that the aftermath of war must of necessity lead to a temporary unsettlement. We are in a world of imperfection, we are desirous of going forward – backwards – (he looks at his notes a little confused) – but other countries are very slow in their progressive notes, but we are Britishers, folk of one common purpose, of goodwill, shoulder to shoulder, hand in hand, lord and labourer, all marching through the highways and the byways of trial. And we will reach the Golden Gate that will open to us, the wonderful mecca of Prosperity, Success and Empire Unity.'

Iago sits down exhausted, wipes his perspiring brow and we all cheer. Again I must say with Hamlet, 'What a wonderful piece of work is man.' Iago collars our votes and leaves us empty-handed, filled only with the inspiration of his fiery peroration.

This kind of comic opera cannot go on for ever. Men keep being made redundant. The machine moves on triumphantly. Men, despite their willingness to do anything for the most modest return, keep getting told 'Nobody wanted today.'

Each year sees the quality of the unemployed changed by the increase in their quantity. A few street-corner louts are of no account, but three million learning to write their name at the labour exchanges became a problem, each chancellor would say 'a thundering nuisance'. They chase about like men gone mad, looking for work, in fact they are losing their eyesight due to the searching. It has gone on, for many, two and three years. Each year emphasises the hopelessness of it all. The rota committees that dish out the few jobs that relief work finds, have now to callously inform the overeager seeker that 'There is no chance for you; men with three years out must have first preference.'

South Wales has had and still possesses the scourge – ten years of it. Tyneside and parts of Scotland followed on their heels and now Lancashire has been seriously in its throes for at least four years. Brightness is still round the corner. From war to peace, from peace to unemployment. The fineness of the underdogs and the unemployed is their trueness to nature's dominant characteristic, the determination to continue in life. Middle-class wallahs and financiers in trouble oft take the coward's way out, suicide; the lowly in the main stick very tenaciously to existence. It is out of such a condition that one loses the manners of a primrose buttonhole, a hungry man becomes an angry man and a little less like a boy of the bull-dog breed.

The early colonists and imperialists who went to America found the native redskins not suitable for their needs. To meet their requirements for slave labour they imported the black man. The native redskins being of no use to them were subjected to a process of gradual extermination, they were kept more or less in restricted reserves. Their means of expression was subdued; now they are in the main creatures of isolation and their fewness makes them curiosities – the policy of their white brothers has meant their dying off. It seems as though such a policy would have merit now as a method of dealing with us no longer profitable beasts of burden.

After all, if we are redundant there is no purpose in our continued existence. It has happened to the horse simply because the machine is more effective; it has happened to the redskin, simply because the 'Nigger' was more effective. It cannot happen to us, possibly the snag is in our numbers, we are a quality in our many-ness. Still I do know now of public assistance committees discussing birth control. Each unemployed man is a backward number, but three million daunts even the daringness of the Churchill-cum-Stamp brigade. Maybe the British method will be a long process of grass feeding, a series of continued percentage cuts into our vitals. I hope they are more sensible, for this would only likewise lead to a continued development of resistance.

The law of the loaf is the law of life – without it one starves, with it one lingers. The common dominant in all species of life is the struggle for survival. Take away the loaf, the means of continuity, and even peaceful blue-eyed Saxon British unemployed will become natural wolves, gluttonous and ravenous, determined to conform to natural law, the law to continue. If the Financial-cum-Bank-cum-Insurance-dictated politicians take away the bread from the boys of the bulldog breed then they will need the combined forces of the four horses of Eucalyptus, the despotism of a Peter the Great and the police system of fascism. Even with all these their days would be numbered. Governments stand with plenty of scope but they must provide bread. They may be composed of shams, or of the best of intentions, of froth or despotisms, still the basis of general society's tolerance is bread. Give to all the loaf of existence and therein lies the hope of life, durability and stability. Nature will, I agree, show its contempt of righteous ethics and idealism by permitting governments to exist that treat minorities indifferently. The essential is: Govern by bread. Some economists will yaw-yaw, with the civilised cuteness of knowing how to conduct the business of a nation, yet I and my kind of countless ignorant, inarticulate flotsam and jetsam know we are in a mess. We lounge and walk, often look for work we now know intuitively is non-existent. We get somehow or other drawn to what is known as 'working for a cause'. The cause of the unemployed, the cause of ourselves, the neglected and the despised, the unwashed, exploited by all political parties – yes, all I say, bar no one. They all take advantage of our misery.

Somehow or other I thought we had taken too little interest in ourselves, had been too content in being appendages for other political parties. I thought we had stood enough, surely we should awaken out of our lethargy, surely if we organised sufficiently our lot would improve.

Together we could make the sleepy council a little active; they could be pushed into finding work. Work, the thing we all looked in vain for. Meanwhile they must be pressed to give us ham and eggs, the scale of the public assistance committee must be raised. So it happened. Similar things were happening in most of the towns and cities, its birth lay in the fact of so many being more or less fed up.

I slipped into it out of my seeing a group of four conducting a meeting. They were trying to show to about six or seven of us who had nothing else to do other than listen, the way to alter things. 'Organise' was the slogan, get together was the method; I joined up, and was invited to an indoor discussion of tactics to be adopted.

Here we drew up all kinds of ambitious schemes: town meetings, deputations to the council, putting forward of all kinds of things we thought of great concern to us and, recognising the need for backing, we set about the task of getting followers.

At our propaganda meetings we at first only got a little lad and a dog. If our audience increased it was generally hostile. Collections we dare not ask for. We could not speak for nuts, we were badly clobbered, we had not that respectable appearance, we were raw and very green. Still we had within our breasts what people call inspiration. This was the urge, the urge out of which all lost and hopeless causes get the sustenance to continue. Laughed at and ridiculed, we were dubbed workshys or idiots, and 'what-can-they-dos'. Slowly and surely we improved, improved to being able to get a platform, perform the crude rudiments of stating our case. It became our existence. Bill would be what we termed 'coming out', that would mean he had spoken some words continuously for fifteen minutes, Joe would get confidence to be the chairman, Frank would be able to conclude with a peroration about the good things that could be if we only got together. Gradually we got better, got wise to the many little tricks of the talkie game, how not to get hoarse, how not to say it all at once, how to dress it up, humour it, get our listeners a little grieved at their misfortunes, indignant at how they were treated, get them optimistic, feeling that something could be done, would be done, and must be done. We grew, we whitewashed the flags with our slogans, as a form of publicity to awaken our fellow sufferers. We painted our posters, became our own sandwich men.

From bell ringing and howling to beautifying public buildings with words, made with what the press called white pigment, we pressed on with our publicity. Interest increased in us. We got our audiences, they listened; and so, now, did the detectives. Bill was ever trying to improve, he started to swallow the dictionary page by page, somehow or other he could not stop, it was words, words, words. He would sit in the library hours upon hours, writing and pronouncing words, then at night he would deliver himself. What a strain he put on himself, underfed, rushing from inarticulateness to eloquence, mastering the fluency of speech, the meaning of words, words, words. More and more Bill swallowed and delivered. The task was too mighty. He nearly conquered; then, snap: he became potty. He flew off at a tangent, he became a reincarnation of a French Revolutionary, made the hottest speech of his speeches. Years of starvation, consuming of words, the fire in his soul, his mind became unbalanced, he left us in a fit of derangement. He was done for, moody and melancholy, never again normal, sometimes walking excessively brisk with eyes staring vacantly about him. Later he was run in for purloining a motor car. Poor Bill, the whitest man I've known.

More harmless than Christ, a life celibate possessing no vice, Bill of all people in prison. There he started to chew the printed regulations. There they found he was gone; after treatment he returned to R—— a strange man, his mind far away from everything, walking about with eyes that never seemed to see, a head always looking upwards and a nervous habit of continually pulling his neck above his collar. Later he again, in an act of unaccountableness, purloined another car, drove it for about a mile, got out and lay on the grass. The police searching for the car, found him. He was arrested muttering: 'There's something doing.' He came up in front of the bench; they did not know him, nor his strangeness; the evidence was convincing, previous conviction mentioned, and lo! a prison medical view of him. It showed him to be an artful dodger, who put the apparent loopiness on so as to get off easily. The bench acting on the evidence before them, administered justice according to their consciences. He went down. It may sound of no account, but knowing Bill as I know him, nothing will convince me of the criminality of his acts; the poor blighter had gone potty. Poverty and overstudy are the causes. He is a case for treatment instead of punishment. Humanity may seem as though its powers of endurance are limitless, but many reach that point when too great an effort sends them over the line. Often, in the case of exceptional, beautiful innocents, they became irresponsible. Bill came out and in a very brief period committed the same act, purloined another car. This time he gets the assizes, eighteen months. POOR BILL. Reader, I cannot dwell on it, there may be some mistake; superficial judgement can commit mistakes. I know Bill was strange, he was once potty (cause: poverty and overstudy) – IS HE NOW SANE? Eighteen months HARD. Bill, the cleanest liver I knew.

So we lost a pal, a lad who had in two years mastered the history of Socialism and memorised all their songs and poetry. We were now getting along, as it were. The Labour Party saw in us prospects of being useful to them, bag carriers, bill deliverers, etc., spade workers to dig the way from one parliament to another. The Communist Party saw an avenue of capturing the movement (yes, we now called ourselves a movement) by co-operation and making it primarily communistic.

So despite our progress, smouldering underneath was the friction of interests – first the cause of the great unwashed; secondly, their potential use as duck eggs to send a man to fight for them sitting on the floor of the House of Commons (e.g., potential rank-and-file workers for Labour Party); thirdly, their stomach hunger made them prospective easy meat for communism which feeds on despair and hopelessness. We managed to keep the Labour Party in its place, but the communists, they need some handling, you can't keep good men down. We kept telling the unemployed, that we all of us should have better treatment, they had nothing to fear, we were just plain blue-eyed Saxons, boys of the bulldog breed like them, but unity would help us all. The unemployed would listen and come again in increased numbers. Every time we got a big crowd, in walked the communists, captured the platforms, scolded us for being blue-eyed Saxons, told us there was no way out but to be Reds. Pandemonium – uproar – desertions, and back again to where we were, slowly building up a consciousness of our own isolated misfortunes. From contempt and ridicule we had changed to the disability of overeager helpers who would give us a handout, by using us to help themselves. There is as much intrigue and strategy in the skirmishing for local dominance as there is in the boloney of world affairs.

On the top of this we had those companionable gentlemen of huge proportions showing their amiable interest at every little pettifogging demonstration we held. They showed us a real brotherly interest, many times following us wherever we went: home, into a shop and so on (I think it is termed 'shadowing'). The poor unwashed, treated with more attention than anyone, and this despite their absence of personality, funds and efficiency! Somehow there seems to be behind the governing mind a recognition that our very poverty makes us a menace; still there is no menace where BREAD is assured. Really these companions are decent fellows, big and strong, possessing an admirable sense of duty, good kind husbands having a love for their children like us, they were human and with it restless. They would see us commit some act, would wonder whether it constituted a breach of the peace and with village sagacity decide not to make a charge but report whatever they saw to the central office.

Fancy a handful of mugs, with no money, little ability and only enthusiasm, requiring much of the time of a few sleuths of rural origin. I wonder why our police system keeps to big men for their work. Big men are I think often like some heavyweight boxers, slow thinkers.

Still they are, at heart, warm and tender, mostly good-humoured babies. They just want to pass the time away serviceably, until pension time comes along, with as little obtrusiveness as possible. I feel sure their desire is for a nice quiet uneventful life of traffic directing, getting up children's treats, saluting the members of the watch committee. Kindness is ingrained deep in their disposition.

There was perhaps good reason for their attention to us, for their perturbation as to our lawfulness, when we pigmies, rats in the alcoves and sewers of poverty, dared to be demonstrative and ironical, as to the good kind honourableness of the men they salute. Different conditions make for different dispositions and viewpoints. They are members of a big machine, one I very much respect because of its perfection of organisation. Any of you tories that think they allow this freedom of speech business to go beyond human tolerance should thank your stars for its efficiency. Slowly but surely they extract teeth for whatever pain you have been caused, Mr Citizen. Slowly but surely, the wings of impertinence, indiscretions and lawlessness are clipped and public acclamation is got for their commendable discretion, tact and restraint (VIDE PRESS). When they make a charge, they are convinced, by their specialist knowledge and practice of law protecting, that the charge is not one based on hazy notions, but based on what is to them convictable evidence.

What is the cause the unemployed stand for? Briefly, it is the fight for the loaf. What are the obstacles to be overcome?

Well, they are numerous, they appear insurmountable, but still noble spirits keep coming and going, each doing something to help to overcome them. The obstacles are: the vote idea (this means deferring your activities to election periods), the political dope with its fraction against fraction, the economical mind, possessed by so many business men, statesmen and rate-saving organisations, the local bye-laws (these tend to restrict your activities, e.g. rights of streets, rights of gathering together, etc.); the laws of the land imposed by Christian men of goodwill, the law's delay, the insolence of office, the proud man's contumely, the rich man's frown, the capitalist's expression of the sanctity of profit, the rights of private property, the crime of theft, the rival organisations who appease temporarily by charity, the leagues for the spreading of alleged economic truths, financed by neutrally minded capitalists, the dishonest feeling that registers itself in your chronic poverty, the slow lethargy, that becomes well-nigh overpowering after months and years of anguish brought on by the whips and lashings of an outrageous fortune, the indifference of humanity to an army afflicted with the leprosy of poverty's indecencies, the suspicion that you may want to mooch a fag from your fellow man.

Have you not seen the *volte face* of the publican, the pal, the parson, the town councillor, the doctor, in fact of nearly everyone, when you approach them in shabby dress, with that look of pinched hard-up-ness, that expression of evolutionary sinking? What do they do? Don't they all seem in a hurry, they want to be going, they are busy, they put up such a frosty barrier that your decaying sociability cannot break through. You are not company for fortune's favourites. I don't blame the men of success, men of happy homes, men of full-fedness. Poverty is a thing that the normal human mind ever shunned. Poverty is leprosy – ugly, nauseating.

This Florence Nightingale stuff, this history of missioners rendering temporary relief to the lepers, the army of good ladies with their parcels in the slums, this visit of the Mayor to the workhouse on Christmas Day, this idea of Sheldon's *In His Steps*, it is all only a perversion of the sum total of man's actions – an admirable one, no doubt, but . . .

The great number abhor poverty, abhor association with it. With righteous indignation they keep aloof from the cess-pool and its contents. The East is East, and the West is West and never the twain shall meet, says Kipling, and like most of his jingo stuff it sings the song of continuity, so let it be. 'I'm a better man than you, Gunga Din.' The East is hunger and despair, the West is the high lights and buoyancy. The clamour and the warmth of one makes for its attractiveness. The naked starvedness of the other makes for its repugnance. What can the dispossessed of jobs and shekels offer to anyone? Brotherhood, companionship, sleeping out, fireless grates, irritated wives, consumptive babies, patched trousers, 'spikes', hopes of a future state, hopes of a deliverance through a path of struggle via the lanes of persecution, imprisonment, riots, police batons and the machine-gun bullets of militarism.

No wonder the sceptic in the crowd looks at the man on the tub and, on seeing him sweat and foam at the mouth, says, 'He must get something for it.' Where in the name of Mother Grady does he get it from? Come on, now, Mr Misanthropist. The law of logic says, you cannot have something from nothing. So it is with the man on the tub. He is a man doing it for nowt. Then I suppose you will say, Mr Misanthropist, 'Well, anybody who will work for nothing will steal.' Yes, he would steal the privileges of the modern Bourbons if only he could get enough thieves of the same kidney to make it accomplishable.

Theft is moral only if it succeeds. Private property stands as a monument to its sanctity and the absence of the same by the poor proves the extent of the robbery. The man on the tub must be looked on as the Dick Turpin of the age of legalised robbery. The age when possession is what it means, the right to hold, protect and endeavour to keep. We have left behind the days of the freebooter, who sacked, collected and passed on, we have come to the more civilised day of systematised plundered monopoly which is founded on annexation.

Profit is the immutable law, the passport of action, the right of the powerful, the dynamic of life, the reward of the squeezer, the harbinger of progress. Profit is the expression of ownership, the law of the club, the jungle, the claw. Skin or be skinned, wonderful skin game, bulling and bearing, ever going on, some rising, some falling. Group against group, nation against nation. Sacred rights, territories, trade monopolies, zones of friction, necessity of defending your ownership. Better ships, more armaments, world competition, the fight for markets, the fight for world dominance, contraction of markets, each country self-sufficing, each country wanting to make the other buy their profit-producing goods. Cut prices, cut wages, cut unemployment benefits. Become efficient, hang humanity, the race is to the men of steel. No slop, no sympathy. World dominance, world power. Oh wonderful man, in apprehension how like a God, a fiction God. And what biblical sanction we have for such tenets.

'It is easier for a camel to pass through the eye of a needle, than for a rich man to enter the kingdom of God.' (Mark x, 25.)

Did not Luke write: 'The beggar died and was carried by the angels into Abraham's bosom; the rich man also died and was buried, and in hell he lifts up his eyes, being in torments . . . But Abraham said, "Son, remember that thou in thy lifetime receivedst the good things and likewise Lazarus evil things; but now he is comforted and thou are tormented".'

We, the unemployed, suffer the worst effects of this skin game, our numbers are constantly being added to. No wonder we get restless. Restlessness born out of the indifference and slowness of the governing classes to effectively assist us.

We got the May Commission, the ten per cent cut, oh yes, everybody got cut, too, but there is a difference: it is inhuman to cut an unemployed man's pay. Why? Because it has never been high enough for modest decencies. We got the means test. That meant that the family had the responsibility of maintaining its unemployed if they had been out over six months. Oh yes, Mr Daily Economist, I know the family affection is warm enough for that. But in most cases a dualism of the wages of those in work and the unemployed members' pay combined only kept the family barely up to the standard.

What are they doing now in those houses with one or two members bringing no unemployed pay in? They are sharing at a common pool that only permits an impoverished standard. I see now, Mr Politician, you have further schemes for economy against us. Do you forget that governments rule by BREAD? The May economies resulted in a lot of hardships for us. They only caused a lot of resentment. There were demonstrations all over the place, and some unfortunately were not on the blue-eyed Saxon bulldog breed lines. The police showed plenty of tact, but the hungry groups of famished men acted like the beasts that poverty makes them. Here and there, there were small riots, disturbances were common. Even our group of half-inchers, more like fogged idealists, got in a scrape. Of course we were guilty: vile language was used, windows were broken, stones were thrown, assaults were committed. A mob was unleashed: it was angry, it was hungry, it had been underfed.

Arrests were made. The evidence and the breaches of the

law justified them. BUT the enforcement of the law does not remove the cause, it merely deals with effects. During days of boom there were no windows broken, no vicious assaults, no howling mob. They were happy rosy-cheeked blue-eyed Saxons. A well-governed society rarely has its laws broken. Happy contented populations are peacefully tranquil. Man in the main only wants to live, a shelter, two or three good meals and nice clean-faced children. The criterion of good government to me must be how full are its gaols. If they are empty, well that can be accepted as contentment, if they are full, it shows the law's inability to adjust itself to Society's requirements.

The social benevolence of this present government is manifested by the number of its offenders in gaol. The politicals that have been put away could have the highest qualities of inflammatory sedition possible, but if you feed the people, you need have no fear. The way to cure unemployment is not putting men away, it is finding the people something to do or feeding them. Well might Caliban utter

> '*For every trifle are they set upon me;*
> *Sometime like apes that mow and chatter at me*
> *And after bite me; then like hedgehogs, which*
> *Lie tumbling in my barefoot way and mount*
> *Their pricks at my footfall; sometime am I*
> *All wound with adders, who with cloven tongues*
> *Do hiss me into madness.*'

# Prison

*But neither milk-white rose nor red*
*May blossom in prison air;*
*The shard, the pebble and the flint*
*Are what they give us there.*
*For flowers have been known to heal*
*A common man's despair.*

BALLAD OF READING GAOL

IMPRISONMENT HAS BEEN A METHOD of curing society's misfits nearly since the days of Adam. We will not go so far back, however, as Daniel in the lions' den; we will rush through our own misfortunes since the days of Elizabeth with their castles and dungeons, no cleanliness – light and air things unknown and methods of isolation, chains, and tortures. In fifteen seventy-seven 'Gaol Fever' was rampant. History records that at 'the Black Assizes' held at Oxford, all the people at that court died inside two days, somewhere about three hundred of them, including the Lord Chief Baron. Speaking of seventeen hundred and fifty, Arthur Griffith says, 'it was common for released prisoners to take back contagion to their homes; and later the Lord Mayor of London, two judges, an alderman, and many of inferior rank, fell victims to the fever . . . Sanitary precautions and rules of action, which are today considered indispensable, were then a dead letter.' James I transported a hundred 'dissolute' persons to Virginia; Cromwell showed his love of fair play to the 'Politicals' by sending them to America. Parliament with its human urge ratified transportation as the law of the land by seventeen-seventeen. Our colonies must be developed. Some gaols were even privately owned, hulks were strewn up and down the Thames. And slowly improvements took place. A luxury building costing half a million was thrown up on a swamp. England's penitentiary, to wit Millbank (1816–1843). This was the prelude to Pentonville. Some luxury! Prisoners died hand over fist in 1823 – it was an epidemic, scurvy and flux. The cause was considered unknown then (even a hundred years before it was common among the Italian peasantry). Enquiries showed they had had their rations cut in two. Despite the efforts at cure, the dying kept going on. Eventually they transferred the prisoners to the hulks. Unfortunately this unfathomable epidemic meant the death of most of them. In those days they knew how to keep order. Under act 7 & 8 G. IV it had become lawful to inflict corporal punishment in serious cases, Griffith describing it thus: 'The whole of the prisoners of the D. ward, to which Sheppard belonged, were therefore assembled in the yard, and the culprit tied up to iron railings in the circle.' 'Having addressed the prisoner,' says the Governor, 'on this disgraceful circumstance, I had one hundred lashes applied by warden Aulph, an old farrier of the cavalry, and therefore well accustomed to inflict corporal punishment, who volunteered his services. The surgeon attended and he being of opinion that Sheppard had received enough, I remitted the remainder of his sentence, on the understanding to that effect with Mr Gregory (the sitting magistrate). The lashes were not very severely inflicted, but were sufficient for example. Sheppard, when taken down, owned the justice of his sentence, and, addressing his fellow prisoners, said he hoped it would be warning to them; he was then taken to the Infirmary.'

A strong force of extra warders were present to overcome the spectators; but all the prisoners behaved well except one who yelled 'murder' several times, which was answered from the windows above, whence came also the cries of 'shame!' Speaking of women about to be sent to penal colonies, less than a hundred years ago, Mrs Fry writes: 'The mode in which the female convicts were brought to embark was very objectionable. They arrived from the country (to Millbank) in small parties at irregular intervals, travelling by stage-coach, smack or hoy, under charge of a turnkey; arriving and coming alongside in a wherry, wayworn and ill, a bundle of sufficient clothing their only provision for the voyage, and accompanied generally by destitute children. In one case the woman arrived, not merely handcuffed but with heavy irons on her legs, which had occasional swelling, and even serious inflammation. Eleven came with iron hoops round their legs and arms, chained to each other. During their journey by coach, they were not allowed to get up or down unless the whole did so together. Some had children to carry but they received no help or alleviation to their sufferings.'

Pentonville, the model prison, was a step for the better, it was the introduction of the solitary. This had to be reduced eventually from two years to nine months. (Nine months was inhuman.)

By 1875 a new prison system had been established. It was, like its pioneer model Pentonville, of the solitary type. Speaking of it Griffith says, 'In our practice today, by a simple compromise, we have nearly solved the problem: we subject our prisoner to solitary confinement for a time, for as long, in point of fact, as by our modern experience we find it feasible without damage to life or understanding' (1875).

Politicals like Michael Davitt and later still the conscientious objectors have done much to change penal methods. Slowly prisons have improved, they have become more scientific; they are not now plague-stricken, nor dark dungeons, nor users of racks. But they are still very severe. Their severity is one of a trained character, you live in gaol and your mind is made to know that you do. Imprisonment today is one of scientific perfected uniformity, a living death. The putting of men away certainly sobers – temporarily at least – their pep. It has an effect on their minds, and the more sensitive they are the more severe is the affliction.

First you are conducted into a patrol wagon or Black Maria. There might be four or five of you in it, and to make the atmosphere cheerful there are a couple of 'slops' inside. You have not seen much of your pals until then, so association becomes welcome. The presence of the slops however acts as a damp rag. You can drop a hint about the liking for at least a last whiff before arriving at the gaol, but stern routine makes the slops deaf, and they just look on like dummies in wax.

You get to the gaol about three o'clock, and find yourselves hustled in. Its first appearance seems interesting. There are about ten closets with seats. You are marched to these and told to sit down. The sitting makes you become isolated; from this you get your first sense of imprisonment; for, though you are all in a row, you have no visual contact with one another; and talking would have to be audible to be effective, so no one has the guts to talk. A bloke with a jingle that cmanates from dangling keys takes us singly to a fat good-humoured gentleman seated at a table. He asks you your name and verifies it by papers the slops have handed in. He tells you that you will be for it if you don't hand up all your fags (which you have not got) and anything that you possess. He warns you that you're likely to be trapped if you become fly, and tells you someone will 'rub you down'. This, I found out, meant 'search you'.

Then the bloke with the jingling noise takes you to another chap, who, being younger, seems more official. He barks out certain questions about your religion, next of kin and such like; and you are passed on still to another chap and told to 'strip and make it snappy'. He also asks questions and happens to have the wrong kind of humour. (I think he must at one time have been a drill sergeant.) 'Have you ever been in before?' 'No, Sir.' (All these fellows are knighted gentlemen.) 'Ugh! You've been neglected,' comes his cheap repartee. He weighs and measures you, then you pass on to the order of the bath. This is a good utility one, but it would send a Palm Olive actress into hysteria. As soon as you have jumped in, there is a tremendous bawling out of 'Hurry along! Hurry along!' by a couple of prisoner bath attendants. You finish as soon as possible and get into your clobber. If you're on remand you can have your own, providing they are not too torn, and also free from vermin; and if you're a first-timer you get a distinction in dress from an old hand. Then you are taken to some cells, deposited in one, and BANG goes the door! In that bang you suffer a thousand shocks that flesh is heir to. It was a knock that made Macbeth fall to pieces; and that BANG is the noise that makes you fall to pieces.

When will the door open again? How long is a minute? or ten? or an hour? or a day? You walk up and down your twelve feet by nine, like Felix. At times your hands involuntarily rise, you face the closed door and thrust a clenched fist towards it. Then you realise you are losing your grip on yourself; and as a puller-up you sit on your scrubbed white buffet and bury your head in your hands. What time is it? What will happen next? How long yet? If you have never dropp'd a tear, your first confinement in a prison cell will try you out.

Slowly, because of time's unbearableness, you take stock of what's around you. The brick walls are lime-washed and have a four-foot-six stone-coloured dado. There's a window of three panes, measuring in all about a yard wide and eighteen inches high at its peak. The window's top is elliptical and behind it are about nine iron bars of sturdy character. To reach the window you would have to stand on your buffet (this is against the regulations), and if you did get up and look out, you would see nothing other than many other windows of a similar block, the block exercise ground, and the huge high outer wall.

Your furniture consists of a buffet, a small stout table, and a washstand, all of which are of white scrubbed wood; on the table is a salt jar, a mug of small pint-size with no handle, and a knife made out of a kind of zinc tin, with a hammered hem to prevent sharpness. In the corner, on the floor, is a wooden soap box and scrubbing brush: on the washstand you've a bowl and a quart water jug. Your pictures are prison regulations, ways of appeal and the privileges of remand. After this scanty survey you return to your Felix-walking backwards and forwards, and every minute you feel like pounding on the iron door. There is a constant struggle between physical-action-and-damn-what-happens on the one hand, and caution, on the other. And I feel sure that struggle must make a man demented. How long is a minute? How long is an hour? When will someone come? Eventually tea time arrives after what has seemed a month, though one has only been about two and a half hours in the prison and only about one in the actual cell.

You hear the shuffle of feet, the methodical unlocking of doors, a pause at each one, and then the awful slam of every door. You are there waiting for the door to open; the key grating in the lock sounds like a Tchaikowsky bar, the door swings open and a warden uninterestedly tells you to put up your mug for your cocoa. You fly for your mug, all fingers and thumbs, and hold it for a fellow prisoner (who acts as a kind of orderly) to pour cocoa into, out of a pail.

Now you get the first lesson, and an effective one too, of prison schooling; for if you don't put your mug at the standard angle and height for the orderly to team* – he teams – and your cocoa is on the floor. Another prison orderly puts in your hand or on top of your mug a lump of dark bread with a dab of margarine sticking on top like a plum on a cake. You then step back, and slam goes the door!

You take this not-too-appetising meal to your table, and, though it is then loathsome (later, hunger makes you enjoy it), for want of something to do, you endeavour to consume

* To pour.

some of it. The cocoa is so nicely made for the palate that no one would ever be able to sell it to the public. The bread is in the same category, and though margarine of the kind that is made palatable by big business is often used in working-class homes, prison margarine at your first tasting of it is utterly distasteful. Eventually you shove about seventy-five per cent of your provided tea away from you, with a feeling of sorrow, melancholia and disgust.

After another seemingly endless period of time there is noise and mobility outside, and you all get let out. Eternity of time may be a term, but if you want to gather its meaning to the full, my dear brother, take your first half-day in a pukka gaol, and you'll realise its immensity. Well, you're out on the landing, and the warder casually barks out, 'Lead off from the left', and away you go in single file. It is the march of the condemned, and you feel it as you pass through endless unlocking and locking of doors until you reach what is the architecture of some Human Satan. By that I mean the centre of the prison. What a knock on a man's sense perceptions! I've been in St Paul's and Westminster Abbey, and by their design I felt my insignificance in relation to the universe or a deity, but a prison centre is a most cruel arrangement, one that gives your psyche such a jab that your stomach sickens and your spine gets a cold shiver.

It is the hub of a living graveyard; there you get a bird's-eye view of the multitudinous revolting monotony. Instead of a chapel in its centre, you see a glass-circled cabin for warders, and you form a ring around it. You look at what you see in fear-stricken amazement, for from the centre are many spokes, like channels or streets, each one possessing rows of uniform doors. Every door is like the others, and each, you know, shuts in one of society's misfits. You look up, and see to each street there is a second and third landing, each with its same uniformity of doors, and a spiral staircase to reach them. All these upper landings have railed fencing, and in case there should be a break-out of a mentally tortured soul, there is a safety net of strong wire netting across the well. So you get your first taste of your environment. This is Civilisation, the compass and ruled lines of a draughtsman, making exact uniformity, each segment of the orange alike, each filled with silent solitary souls. Damn the psychic vice of such a designing brain. Little need now for flogging, dungeons and foulness. You can do it with clean air and light. Just make everything the same – so silent – so solitary – so inhumanly civilised. Slowly comes your turn to go up to a table on which lie bundles of books.

You give your name and get your bundle, plus a card which classifies you, stating your name and religion, conviction or remand, and the block you are to be deposited in. Then you fall in single file, toeing a ring, and await developments. When the last of the prisoners has got his card and bundle, there's a count to see none have vanished. Then the same indifferent impersonal chirp, 'Lead off by the left', and you move again in single file to one of the spokes (streets or blocks) that shoot off from the centre, you walk along the block, the first one halting at the farthest empty cell and then each at a cell behind.

You are ordered to place your cards in the frame outside the door. Then the warder – from now on called screw – looks up and down to see us all in miscellaneous forms of attention, and again indifferently chirps 'Into your cells.' Once again there's a rhythmic banging of doors one after the other, and the grating of the key. You look around at your home, and find it like the one you left behind just after tea with the addition of a bed board of three planks' width and nearly seven feet long, with two batons underneath to raise it about three inches from the floor. In the corner is about a pound of oakum to help you pass your time away.

I look at my books: Holy Bible, a book of texts, and a Christian sermon in story form about sinners at the cross-ways. Being on remand, I have also two other books, one about some punitive gangster in Klondyke, and the other the love of good women. I tried to read but it was impossible. My eyes saw the letters, my mind made them into words, and then they became meaningless again. I gave it up, turned to the oakum, and started tearing it up into strands. I had for a neighbour a 'regular', who started tapping on his side of the cell wall, and eventually I plucked up courage to tap back, so killing a portion of our seemingly everlasting time. Then I heard him banging his bed board on the floor of his cell, and promptly took the hint, did the same, and got down to it.

What a night! Nervous perspiration, and sleep constantly broken by primeval jumps of subconscious fear. How long is a minute? How long till morning? At long last I am asleep only to be aroused by the noise and commotion caused by the other prisoners picking up their bed boards and leaning them on the cell walls. It seems remarkable what knowledge is possessed by blind men of what is taking place; and prisoners are the same. By noise and movement you gather what is afoot. Out of the low-lying bed I bound, fold up in amateurish fashion the three blankets and two coarse narrow sheets, put the bed on board against the wall, and hang the bedding over its sides. With alacrity I hasten to wash, and then I find my cell door open and my fellow luckless tramping with their chambers and water jugs to the wash place and lavatory. Mimicry being as natural with man as sheep, I fall into line, and bring back a filled water jug and clean chamber. Then once again the screw bangs the cell door. I hear my neighbour old-timer scurry about his cell, and presume he is giving it a clean-up; so I begin to do likewise. Then breakfast comes, and now from the experience of the previous tea time I savvy the ropes. I stand with enamel plate in one hand and mug in the other. When the door is opened, I hand the plate to one prison orderly, who ladles out the prescribed measure of what's termed porridge; and hold the mug at the right height and angle for the other to team tea into it out of his pail.

The screw dumps me the dark bread with the lump of margarine on the top, I step back, and bang again goes the door. So comes my first experience of prison breakfast. I have sulked at the tea-time grub and am faced with as unenticing a grub for my morning repast. I try a spoonful of porridge and it seems repugnant; so the bread is tackled and half of the issue is consumed. Then a little later the doors are opened and there is a scurry, this time to empty the slops of cell-cleaning and the little pot-washing. When I return, the door is once again slammed and I discover that I've left the plate of porridge untouched, and consequently unwashed. 'Is it a crime?' I wonder. I begin to worry, and to settle the torment, set about scroffing it cold and lumpy. It was as loathsome as castor oil would be to a kiddie, but 'The plate must be made clean,' thinks I.

After this comes once again the opening of cell doors. 'All outside with your sheets, pillow case, books, and history card.' We are to be examined by the doctor. He sees you are clean, sounds your heart with a trumpet and asks you if you are feeling all right. You reply dispassionately 'Yes, Sir', and all's over. It takes about a couple of minutes per man. This being got through, you take your turn at seeing the parson. How different he is from the one we know of and associate with at christenings and weddings, or the associate of old women's sewing classes! He is hardened with ministering to society's bad lads, and looks on your introduction as a formality. He does not overdo the Jesus stuff. There is something about him you do not like. It is that he seems to be a power, an authority, whom getting at cross words with would lead to your disadvantage. There is also something to commend about him. It is the absence of any pious acidity. In fact he attempts, despite the drabness of the atmosphere, to be a humorist.

After this there's still another parade – the governor's – with some sort of committee looking on. I don't know exactly who appoints this committee, but I've a sort of an idea they are there to see fair play. You have been schooled up by the screw how to act, and you follow the previous prisoner, you go in, spring to attention, and say your name, age, religion. The governor looks at you, repeats your name, age and religion, and tells you how long you have to do. He turns to the 'Gentlemen' who are seated sideways to him, they give you the once over and nod, and he says 'All right.' You about turn and walk out of their presence. When all this red tape is completed, you have found yourself placed by the screws to various groups according to length and kind of sentence or awaiting trial. Each group has its own pet keeper, and then comes a chief warder, who, holding some regulations in his hand, reads them out. They are supposed to be what you have to conform to. Well, whatever they were, I heard some noise come from him, but not a single word could I make out. He just ripped it out parrot-like, and when he'd finished, you were no wiser. It was sheer martinet staccato pistol-rapping monotonics. I've heard paper lads shouting their wares, and only the fact that they had papers in their hands made me know they were selling them. It was the same with this verbal rendering of prison regulations – just a meaningless noise from which you gathered that if you did this and not that you would be for it.

Away you go with your little group to the block provided for your class of offender. There were ten in our little lot, ten remanded, ten still in suspense. Our journey takes us to the centre again, and then our screw shouts to the screw who is on duty in B Block: 'Ten coming up.' Up we go, up the steel spiral staircase round and round, up and up, each turn and each step up making us see the efficient similarity of everything, doors for hundreds upon hundreds, landings upon landings, blocks north, south, east and west, of the centre. The centre, the hub from which all movement action or life in any of its spokes could be seen.

Up we go, arriving at the top landing. Here our new chum, the block screw, our own special one, till we go out, is awaiting us. Here we are, settled for a time, our spiritual home. From our buffet, looking through our respective windows, we being now high up, you can see something. Chimney stacks belching forth smoke, how welcome you are, smoke is at least movement. It uncurls itself, the wind makes it move towards the west; still despite this forceful master it does have expression, it fluctuates, rebels, climbs, waves, climbs and falls again. The mind reflects its conditional being; smoke of no ordinary importance becomes the undreamt expressive fantasies of the subconscious scope for creation. Mr Designer, you overlooked that; still, Civilisation, you may make amends by taking away this antiquity of smoke. Modern science will supplant you with electricity.

Good fortune is still with us; it is now near dinner time. One hears the roll of a travelling carrier, on which are the cans containing the dinners. Key in lock, cell door opens, the screw motions a debtor prisoner to give you a can, and another pushes the carriage towards the next cell, and bang goes your door. You look at what you have got, it is a can, like a clean one used by painters, minus the wire handle, it possesses a lid which when reversed sits in the can and becomes a convenient plate.

In this there is about a large spoonful of beans or cabbage. When you lift the lid out, you find three or four small spuds and a fair-sized slice of bully beef and possibly a piece of concoction made from fat suet and flour. Of my spuds I found one broke, one was valueless because of its black badness, one half and half, the other two quite sound and good. The suet concoction was hopeless in my present not-too-famished state, the beans and the bully were O.K. in every respect. I found a relish for them and commiserated with myself for the loss of the spud and a half; after a while the door opens, you've cleaned your plate, and you take your leavings and return with water for future cleanings.

Our friend the screw deems it his duty to pay you a visit. It amounts to this, 'No talking, keep your cell spotlessly clean and give no trouble.' After this intimation, he shows you once how to fold your bedding, and you are then supposed to be schooled up; if you come unstuck you'll most likely be 'for it'. So I look, examine closely the bedding folds, try it a time or two, and hope when morn comes I have not forgotten; few do forget. How long is a minute, how long an hour, how long a day? With Felix-walking up and down, thinking how to keep out of 'being for it', at last the time for exercise comes. The doors open, you're out, led off by the left, descend to the bottom, outside door unlocked and you pass to the exercise ground.

You have most likely seen a dartboard, well an exercise ground is similar. It is rings inside one another. These rings are made of stone flags; it is like walking on the flags in the street only you walk round and round. The young and energetic walk on the outer rings briskly, and the proportionately less mobile crawl on the graduating inner small rings. The energetic squad on the outer ring move round and round ever turning to their right, those moving in the ring just inside of them, walk the reverse way, those inside them keep walking right and those who are the slowest crew crawl along the innermost ring continually turning left. You see you are always walking away from the men inner to you. This prevents it being the companionable stroll of four deep.

To check you from holding conversation with the men traversing the same ring as you, you are spaced about three yards away from one another. As a further precaution two screws are watching you from points opposite to each other. The most you can snatch with your fellow prisoner is about two words a stroll round, and by the time you've finished a sentence, your exercise time is about up. If you happen to get too near the man in front, the screw puts up his hand and you then have to stop until there's a sufficient distance between you to prevent talking.

The exercise ground is the one bright spot in prison, despite its arrangement to prevent it developing into a forum. To be able to step out twice a day into the fresh air and see only nature's cap above is a boon that is conceded because of necessity. It is the thing looked forward to and it is as much a tonic as is the Mediterranean to the dyspeptic overfeds. Your work consists of mending or making mail bags. (Remands, if sensible, volunteer to do some; work kills time, time is the affliction.) I have seen some terribly swollen puffed and needle-pierced fingers from this occupation. There is also weaving of a kind done by some prisoners and of course many other various jobs, necessary to prison management. Now, dear reader, I will not tire you with further movement of prison routine. I have just given you twenty-four hours of it. Remands stay until time for trial, others till their time expires. But it becomes one long period of slow monotony. One surprising thing about these men put away is, there is nothing in their general appearance to suggest their being criminal-minded. Physiognomy shows in them nothing of the Charlie Peace countenance or the Tussauds chamber of horrors. They seem such a crowd of humans that might have been gathered up indiscriminately. (Some good-lookers, some bad.) Most of them, however, have been in before and take it as part of their lives, some of them hold the view that previous conviction is in itself circumstantial evidence of guilt. Their principal grudge is against the law that empowers the authorities to put them away for being incorrigibles, a system which – they claim – allows anyone with a grudge against them to rush them in whenever trade is slack. From what little I know of the Police system it is as I have said before, slow but sure; charges are made only after convincing evidence. In and out seems to be their lot. I am afraid that most of them are treated very harshly in so far as their success from crime is grossly outweighed by the sentences they receive when caught and I fear they are caught very frequently. They are society's outcasts and too well known. Many of them think themselves smart, but inwardly they know it is a mug's game. Still after all, my dear Christians, they are only the petty criminals of society, mostly created out of a position of poverty, and inability to capture life's loaf in the sweet pacific way of honest toil.

The Bishop, the Banker, the large-scale Landlord, the Company Director, and the business man, need break no law of parliament's making, in order to get their temporary needs met. They are the honest men, who are freed from the temptation, by the possessing of ham and eggs *ad lib*, and they know ye not, Mr Desirer of Succour. Their distant forefathers have either been successful in fighting for some corrupt or extravagant King or throwing in their lot with the Church by law established, or receiving out of the plunder of the reformation some of the land confiscated because we are told it was not put into proper use.

The crime of theft is a condition arising out of the inequalities of social position. It is righteous when the thieves are sufficiently dominant to legalise their actions, and even when it interferes with the legalised sanction of individual possession. The accident of birth and opportunity decide when one is a decent, model pattern, good-living, God-fearing, lump of rectitude, *OR* a slick-fingered, begging-letter-writer, butcher's meat stealer, foxy trickster, or highway-robbing violent piece of debasement. Opportunity can make goodness easy, but being in the dark alcoves of society's muck heaps makes entering prisons practically a certainty.

To return to my cell mates: I found them in the main decent comrades. They cheer you up; despite the fact they know that you, being a first-timer, will most likely get off better than they, they are helpful in putting you wise as to how to make your lot easier, and their many little acts of friendliness make you realise they are as good as you are.

There are just two more things worthy of mention: one is church service and the other the callousness of punishment for little nothings. Going to church is a Christian method for the improvement of the individual. In private life you can please yourself, but in gaol it is compulsory. I don't know that the atheist objects very much to this infliction, for after all anything is better than being penned up in a cell. Away you go, with your bible and hymn book, and I should think the average parson would be filled with joy if his little bethel had such a packed appearance. Somehow one senses the mixedness in the worshippers. Some have the sinner's compassion, and in such a holy place, the power of many voices hymning the praises of the Lord and his Goodness, brings tears trickling down their cheeks. Others treat it as all in a day's march, and with lusty lungs belch out the fervent chants as the physical need for the use of the lip and tongue. Others, again, keep to the hymnal tune, but put there words that are not in the book and so make the means of getting a chat with their penitent mates. Others there are who just rise and sit as the ritual of the service demands, but amid it all show a stiffness amounting to disgust. Placed here and there are the screws, trying to fathom the phenomena of what is Christian propriety or what is 'working the oracle'. I am afraid they have a difficulty and most likely mistakes are made when some are caught and are reported to the Governor.

I used to think there was nothing beautiful about a Church or Altar, but by comparison with what is ugly, even Churches and Altars become beautiful. The few flowers that were present, made a great impression after my few days of barrenness; the gothic windows and the stencilled relief of religious symbols made quite an entrancing feast for my hungry eyes. The white, yes, pure whiteness, of the parson's surplice became a nutritious purity to which my aesthetic mind responded, hungering in the drabness of the coarse unbleached sheets of a prison bed. There is something about those services. It arises out of the liberty to function, it is outside the pale of academic training. It is the expressive soul of man, the retarded genesis reborn, it is reminiscent of the Volga Boatmen, it is born of being assembled after weeping in isolation, born of the knowledge of going back to your cell, it is the form of being permitted (this being a Christian service) the vision of a frugal refinement after cultural barrenness. All the lot put together makes for a psychic phenomenon that is more divine than a King's coronation service.

Now for punishment: it is as though scientific minds of educated men had not done enough in their designing and regulating of prison life. The formula is one of being 'Had up in front of the Governor'. You generally get some of your remission marks knocked off, and afterwards may be put on bread and water. The limited diet (though just sufficient) that hunger compels you to eat is, for punishment, taken away from you.

Bread and water to men who eat up even their prison rations amounts to inhumanity, and such treatment for petty offences is cruel. It may seem little or nothing to you in your armchair, but if you saw the face of the bloke who has been doomed to it, you would think it had slipped, and if you saw him after his three days, you would see the change it had brought upon him, he has become sour and ravenous. Bread and water, when one has been having hardly enough before, is no joke.

What sort of civilised action is such callousness? Why, every housewife knows that contentment is brought about by 'feeding the brute'. Prison food is meagre and when you take that away you take the last straw from the poor blighter. It is a punishment that eats into his bones. Oh, society, don't you know that hungry men are angry men and hunger's torments are worse than Dante's 'Inferno'?

You must reason by likeness and difference. An overfed man of leisure, may take up a course of fasting and find it does him good, but a hungry man, made more hungry by bread and water, suffers untold agony. Untold agony for what crime? Being found with a bit of tobacco dust in his cell. Man gets the dummy teat when a babe, swaggering sticks and rock as a boy, and smoking becomes the evolutionary sequence at manhood. Its habitual use makes him its slave, so much so that in prison by some process of magic he manages to get possession not of tobacco, but DUST. The scrapings up of waistcoat pockets of new entrants is somehow smuggled around.

After undergoing the quakings of a regular vigilant search

(being rubbed down), suffering the rat-like darts of the eyes of trained detectors he is 'found out'. Found out doing something that is life's custom – then bread and water. The same applies to speaking: bread and water, the powerful medicine to cure ill behaviour. Just imagine: How long is a minute? an hour? How long are three days? Three days on bread and water. Think of it, you with your indifference and 'do them good' philosophy. Think of it when your stomach aches after gluttony on Sunday night!

What is bread and water to you, when you are in a blue dilemma, wondering what to choose from the menu of your favourite restaurant. If they offered it as a light dessert, of course you would choose it. Thus as Bobby Burns says, 'Man was made to mourn.' He can mourn through the whole three days, but the civilised makers of regulations never hear him.

As you know, imprisonment is a punishment that reduces crime by its deterring effects. That is why a man becomes an habitual member of the prison class! It deters him by being his ever-open door! Oh, the blinking farcical tragedy of it! A life of deadness, restriction, drabness and sewing classes. A life of reading Holy Bibles, limited feeding and screw vigilance. A life full of scope for personality (what hopes), one calling for ambition, one tending to prune the Pygmalion crudeness with the cultured forks of uniformity, par excellence! Iron bars and sturdy doors.

Gentle Jesus, meek and mild, treat me as a little child.

Though I have erred, show me by love, that goodness is the great thing, God! As I fall sometime in the dark, do not shout as dogs do bark, give me sympathy and example, so that in your steps I will surely trample. Spare the rod and save the child, imprisonment is bleak and punishment wild.

# They Call Themselves Comrades

TO FILL IN THE VOID brought on by being placed on the dole I must do something. What? Analyse society as a mild diversion. How interesting, what problems, how easy the solution, 'if only people *will* be sensible'!

Socialism the way out, the pill for all society's ailments. Still, what a vague term. But what a disease, how contagious it is, the source of sustenance, religion, hope, and insouciance. Still I think its study and the pleasure derived out of it have in the main outweighed its discomforts.

First comes the vague notion that all is not well in the state of Denmark, then follows the determination to be a rebel; this often resolves itself into nothing more disturbing than a Sunday-school wallah committing himself to a twopenny damn. Many are the rebels I know, whose rebellious activity amounts to nothing more than attendance at a

Labour brotherhood, a sort of pleasant Sunday afternoon, where you bellow out 'England Arise'. Still I know of others of darker hue, but perhaps just as lovable.

They are hatless and suffer from cerebral fever; they look highbrow and sordidly live on economic rigidity. Marx, Dietzgen and Engels are their food and they eat it up like gluttons. They play cat and mouse with their mongrel brothers who feed on the *Daily Mail*.

Oh, Mr Fair-Play-and-all-for-a-reasonable-tolerance, don't cross swords with them. They will make you look what you are, a fool, and they will delight in the annoyance they cause you. They possess none of man's frailties, such as having a tanner on a horse, being a sport, or indulging in carnival sangfroidness. These things are 'capitalist dope'.

I mixed a great deal of my time amongst these overripe single-trackers, they lack human nature. It is not that they are braver or more sturdy than those outside their province or more likely to tear asunder the pillars of capitalism. They are merely book socialists, their ferocity is confined to the iron rigidity of terminology. Really they are as useful, but in an opposite sense, as a group of feminine cissies when playing cave-man stuff. If you asked them the reason R.I.P. is placed on gravestones, they would say it was to commemorate capitalist Rent, Interest and Profit.

How wise they think themselves discussing 'The relationship of neolithic man to the modern conception of violence'. You meet them in Socialist groups and N.C.L.C.

classes; they have a fixed positive for everything. Their dogmatic emphasis would outdo any Irish Catholic when he is postulating his certainty of Holy Michael. They are, though claiming to be 'class-conscious', really members of cults.

Their lectures are parrot-like and have mathematical precision. To them Bill Shakespeare would be taboo, Tay Pay O'Connor oratory would be sabotage. History is just to emphasise the obvious fact that the 'haves' some time ago diddled the 'have nots', and its purpose is in the last analysis proved conclusively and indubitably to be 'That the only remaining class to rise, will rise', and so become dominant in the we-are-the-boss stakes.

What a language they have! Henries* are known as proletarians; prosperous idlers, alias gentlemen, are christened bourgeois. They throw the word 'Revolution' about, with greater nonchalance than a juggler does cannonballs. Imperialism is another word they fall into using often, it stands for slave-driving in 'away matches'. It seems that having robbed 'Henry' at home of his shirt, they swap it to the South African 'nigger' for a diamond as big as a mountain.

The 'rentier' class is a term applied to those who are accredited with more houses than they can conveniently live in. These humanitarians, with pious goodness, let to the aforementioned good-looking 'Henrys' their overplus of uninhabitable residences, at very immodest rents.

* 'Henry Dubbs' is a popular nickname for the exploited working man.

Surplus value is another bright idea. It covers all the hard-earned profits of the capitalist and so compensates him for his many investments that show calls. There it is, surplus value. You the working class must give surplus in order to satisfy the man-with-the-big-belly, fat cigar and tall shiner. The more you can give him the better he likes it.

'Dictatorship of the Proletariat' is what they scream out. Fancy, Henry, you with your humility and philanthropy, dictating how things shall be done. I only know you dictating at home, lambasting the missus and pummelling the kids. Here is a chance for you. Dictating to the Boss, whom you revere and lickspittle, kicking him up the posterior, the object the sun shines on. 'Swipe me, guv'nor,' I hear you say, 'We are British and don't hold with those continental ideas.'

'International solidarity' is a thing to strive for, but whenever one or two dogs of party fractionism meet for common action, they nearly always snarl and chew one another up.

Nevertheless, the teachings of Marx, Dietzgen and Engels, and latterly Lenin, are having some effect on thought. Even though '*Laisser Faire*' is dying only slowly, the organic view of Society is coming. Man is becoming recognised as a conditioned animal, class antagonism is being discerned, and socialists, despite their desire for 'the inevitable gradualism of evolution', are constantly being compelled to revert back to the 'Marxian Bible'.

We see the impossibility of trade union benefits emancipating the ever and ever growing redundant working class;

the sickness and burial funds have to pay more and more 'due regard to economy', the day of social reform, step-by-step concessions from the successful British capitalist, all this is slowly freezing up. The beautiful carrot of social legislation, dangling in front of the labouring donkey is now only a radish. The donkey is less eager to move towards it and instead of this subtle method to create mobility in him, there is becoming now exposed a driver with whip in hand.

Let us, without prejudice, take a visit to the English army waging war against capitalism. There is the I.L.P. They talk about their party as being their 'Spiritual Home', most of them never miss a meal or appear down in the mouth. This is perhaps done by being careful (common thing amongst all working pecks who have never become really broke). They have branches and club houses all up and down the country, most of them are very nice, but there is generally no bar (this shows an absence of Tory psychology). Though numbered by their fewness they manage to keep a condition of solvency by subscriptions and possessing a few middle-class members who cough up now and again, to show their sympathy for uplifting the working man.

Their work is mostly propaganda and hope in parliament, given the right number of the right kind of M.P.'s. They used to add to this by being an appendage to the Labour Party, this amounted to doing all the spadework – bill delivering, canvassing, and going round with the bag. NO job was or is too humble for them, providing it does not entail physical clash with the forces of law and order. They care little or nothing about high office. (This used to work O.K. with the trade unionists and Labour limelight seekers who, from a sense of duty to oblige, became the candidates and sometimes successful standard-bearers.) Still, even the leading Labour dodgers had, if they wanted the I.L.P. mugs to get them in, to recognise that the I.L.P.'s were the blue bloods of socialism.

They are the people trained and bred to bestow the misfortunes of socialism on the colliers and weavers, despite the latter's colossal gross ineptitude. Kid an I.L.P.'er that his is the butter brand of socialism, that all others are margarine, and he will work until you are emancipated: then if you like you can give him and England's toilers the go by – à la Ramsay Mac and good old Philip.

They stand for a revolution of the mind, they support this by giving the bird to all action of a more violent character than attending orderly meetings. Mostly the younger members are hatless (this is proof of their desire for liberty). Open necks are encouraged, but they have ceased to sport red ties.

They manage, by their respectability and spadework, to create an impression of being somebody who has to be recognised in the body politic. This amounts to nothing more than a public tolerance of the bandying about of the sacred letters I.L.P. Personally I dub them the Inflated Little Pawns. Even though now they are at variance with the party they have helped to make (the Labour Party), out of their womb has come some of the finest climbers I ever saw. These have given utterance to the most inspiring speeches heard. Still you must remember that speeches can be easily reconciled with minds, and as such, they are as helpful as an inoculation against poverty, as is Christian Science against ultimate death.

Some of their star propagandists talk the head off a Giraffe, aye even the neck as well (many have left them high and dry and are now personalities in the Labour Party). Then with a bit of sob poetry and visions of a beautiful idealistic, utopian future, they send the dull-witted unfortunate victims of capitalism's lunacy home – hopefully to wait until the High Priests decide which shall be the particular day when they will inaugurate their 'Socialism in our time'. If they follow their normal traits it will have to be permanently postponed because other than Sundays they seem to be working.

So much for the daffodils. Now, Mr Gardener, let us have a look at the stinging thistles.* This is termed the virile group, it is hated and possesses a counter-hatred. It preaches without apology the gospel of no compromise, and rouses discontent to its maximum capacity. It came into prominence after the successful revolution of the brothers in Russia, and by nineteen-twenty-one had a party organisation. This was mainly composed of left-wingers and Marxists who

* The Communists, 'à la guillotine'.

found no scope in the older socialist-cum-labour parties for their livelihood or political conceptions. It first insisted on its members pledging themselves to a life of warfare against constitutionalism, and enforced a rigid discipline to ensure same. If you desired to be a half-incher and having of ham and eggs under capitalism well, you didn't become a party member. Still you could have contact of a less strict infection in one of their more elastic subsidiary organisations. Party membership demanded giving your life for the struggle against capitalism. I think that many of their members have signed their enrolment forms glibly and so hamper the strength of the movement. The movement stands for revolution, revolution with disturbance and violence, but wails like blazes at its persecution at the hands of the constitutionalists.

They are mostly in deadly earnest, but being infants they have been up to the present easy prey for the highly trained, seasoned henchmen of the governing class. They early started by their fractious work to put the Labour Party right and the Labour leaders out. For this good service they were dubbed disrupters and fired; the same happened in their trade unions.

So driven to splendid isolation they went out to the street corners and market squares, delivering their disruptive declamations to all who by their poverty had to listen. (Instead of drinking beer or going to the pictures.) What a training ground it has been! They have in a few brief years practically made the open spaces their monopoly by right. In the contests between this platform or that, they have won hands down. How?

First, the advantages of being outlawed by the other socialist groups. This permitted them to have open Mulligan's rules. (By that I mean, do what they like; there was no need to consider this Labour tin god's feelings or that trade union bureaucrat's sensitiveness to criticism.) They could get on with the job unfettered. Slandering all and sundry was made acceptable to their poverty-stricken listeners by their dogmatic assertion that they, the working class, are the cream of the milk jug.

Yes, by their tenacity and memories of others having risen on the backs of the workers, they have captured the squares and the gutters, once the preserves of the Labour Party. They are theirs now by the right of conquest and effort. The others have lost them by indolent sloth and their pacific slumber in offices and clubs. They attempt, beside their main plank of denunciation, to organise through the medium of Soviets (committees). I have laughed my sides sore at the results of some of these efforts. Anything and everything that is going calls for the setting up of a committee. To show you what I mean I will refer you to a town branch I know of. Its membership was never above twenty, yet it set up at least twelve committees.

Social, agitation and propaganda, piecers' protection, F.O.S.R., Meerut Prisoners, W.I.R., N.U.W.M., W.S.F., three ward committees, two factory cells, and a municipal campaign committee. At least twelve distinct committees, a party membership of twenty with the addition of whomsoever they could get from outsiders. (Outsiders who are sympathetic to the party but not whole-hoggers, could be encouraged into membership of a subsidiary committee.) Such ambition kept the whole of the party busy all the time attending committee meetings and none of the world knew of their existence. Of these committees only the propaganda and the N.U.W.M. survived – even the N.U.W.M. was a bit wobbly whenever the communists were in the majority. It took this branch of weeny starved immature crude humans all its time to make a big tub-thumping noise without being too ambitious.

Nevertheless I think the shop committee movement will come, even the T.U.C. adopted it once, and then, as they do with most things, dropped it. There's one thing I learned about the party. It is, their earnestness, their zeal and sacrifice; also the readiness to admit the making of mistakes. Mistakes they keep on repeating, however. That is, being in too big a hurry. How proletarian! They are young, a reincarnation of the old Pioneers.

Still, I found them very difficult to live with. Their fractious work with its block effect of carrying a decision and of shouting the others into submission makes one chuck up the sponge and cease to function on their subsidiary bodies. They are indeed hot stuff. They are ever ready to dub you reactionary. The fact that you are not a party member puts you in a position of suspicion and distrust. This form of procedure makes them the dwarf party who never grow up. They have far-reaching influence, everyone knows their message, everyone knows their slogans, but very, very few bite. A few drop in, but a few drop out. It is the party for Spartans.

However their lack of mass membership is not unusual nor over-important. Most movements are but the actions of small minorities, who shout like hell and the man in the street hears; and if they shout long enough and often enough and drown everybody else's shouting they believe it. Public opinion is really the voice of the *Daily Mail* and the *Daily Worker*. Their respective circulations about represents their number of adherents. Now let us look at the Labour Party, the mighty giant built up from the cap wearing 'Keir Hardies'. It is now the embodiment of hundreds of thousands of workers, who have been trained to wait patiently and constantly give presents and stipends galore to the bureaucrats, the giving of which makes the rank and file applaud ferociously, knowing they are giving their employees and their kin a real good time. They progress by their ineptitude. The bugs at the top know something. They know that the working lamb wants to be peaceful with the naughty capitalist lion, so they try their best to make the lion realise it. Now and again, when the lamb is feeling sore with the lion's scratch, they resort to scolding the lion and telling the lamb that the claws of the lion are O.K., but they must change the lion's heart. Still, methinks the lion's *heart* is alright; if it had a few less sharp *teeth* and *claws* it might be better. One misguided worker said 'Shooting was too good for it.' Nature is nature, and a sickly lion roars o'er the empire jungle and according to 'Old Moore' the lamb jumps over the moon.

They – the Labour Party – with their methodist personnel, stand for a change of hearts, a give-and-take sportsmanship. Westminster is the goal to aim for – I wonder how they would deal with a modern Guy Fawkes. Evolution and constipation must be tried with constitutional limitless endurance. Pin-stripes and black cloths must replace fustians. Legislators must be trained and the etiquette of a buffoon's ritual mastered. The fusty acts passed 1616 B.C. must be carefully examined before being repealed and then the capitalist must be slowly and (to him) almost unnoticeably taxed out of existence, with compensation for what pain it causes him. Under no circumstances must the blue and white be deleted from the Union Jack; our God must remain; and the Bishop must take more interest in the poor.

Of course they satisfy no one but themselves. They are mucking about in the garden of quackery, giving as much as the chancellor draws in without extra taxation and ever trying to keep at the parliamentary pay table themselves. Make them Under Secretaries and they go daft in their proudness at being members of 'His Majesty's Government'. By jove, it does buck them up, the honour is nearly as great as the increased screw. Of course they pay tribute to all the bill deliverers for putting them there, but they somehow become less clamorous demagogues the longer they hold office. Therein perhaps lies the nutriment of the starved socialist plant. It is fostered and grows amid the soil of poverty and hopelessness. Change the soil to the fertile cakes of privilege and the plant starts to bring forth flowers of satisfaction, whose rosy hues make joy and happiness to the stems that bear them while the ugly impoverished brother looks on with eyes of envy and scorn and comes out with damnable jibes about selling the pass and being sabotagers.

The Labour Party is proud of its attracted nobility, any turncoat from other camps is welcomed, feted and made a bigwig. Outside the few early birds (old men and women) who have mastered the art of keeping on its whirl in the whirl, its chief wire pullers are becoming more and more middle-class climbers and disgruntled Liberals. The pen is now truly an instrument of labour and the spade is now the 'Joker'. Still methinks they mean well and do well by us. We must thank them for the sunshine, for our babies and certainly for our wonderful English mother-in-laws. They stand on the foundation stone of democracy, a democracy of painfully shallow plates. Any of life's successfuls will have from them due tribute. Their candidates nod and smile, and the sociable Henry wears out his pencil putting up his cross. Crosses are symbolic of the crucifixion; and it means that for many. The innocent carpenters of the twentieth century are nailed to the wood of the law's delay by the insolence of the Labour Party's office.

I do not think one could touch most Labour M.P.'s for much. You most likely would get a nice-worded letter for a reply. I remember when we were a young Labour group. We wanted funds to set us going. We wrote to a Labour M.P., one we thought had youth at heart. 'Of course he would come.' He came, did his stuff, spoke so eloquently that the collection realised thirty shillings. 'What are your expenses, Mr M.P.?' 'Three guineas,' says he. We scratched our heads, and paid him on a commission basis, twenty-five bob. To meet the cost of the hall we had to levy ourselves. Many of our lads worked a full week in the rain for twenty-five bob and coughed up their humble tanner to make us solvent. He, the M.P., had been to two meetings nearby the same week. Still, we must admit they are prepared to go on and on and on, fighting for redress for the poor, fighting for humanity and decency. Yes, fighting ceaselessly, on the floor of the House of Commons. Fighting with chosen words, Aldermanic posture and always remembering, despite the heat of the battle of words, that their opponents are like themselves, honourable members, honourable gentlemen, aye, even 'Right honourable gentlemen'.

They now find horn-rims an advantage in the fight; the stimulating effects of the alcoholic parliamentary bar and sometimes the levee knee breeches give them more freedom and strength in their wordy wrestles. These heavyweight class contests are, like their programmes, figments of the mind, a mental creation, a thesis, a piece of illusion to lead to delusion. In the words of the tory working man, 'a bloody sham'. As G.B. Shaw says, the balloon goes up every five years; it doesn't matter much who is in the basket. Transport House! What an achievement! On, noble trade unionist, to further glories!

Trade unionism! what a struggle to establish it. Dorset labourers, dockers' fights for recognition, railwaymen's struggles for betterment and so on, even black Fridays and general strikes (one). What victories could each place on its banners! What struggles in the past they waged! Now the banners are mostly dirty and dusty, and are barely seen even on May days. In 1920, you had six and a half million members (good old Dorset labourers); in 1932, you had shrunk to under four millions (good old rationalisation); and, temporarily at least, your future activity seems confined to ambulance work. You have by your present organisation little scope for strikes or industrial friction, you are in the groove of conciliation, adjustments and inertia. Your main mission is put and take. The member pays or puts so much a week when he is in clover, and takes out so much a week when he is badly or too old for the benevolent gaffer to exploit him. That briefly is now the purpose of trade unions. Sick and accident benefits, superannuation and death benefits. May you all live long enough to draw your death benefit. Pay up my lads, and we will treat you fair.

Incidentally they pay men to be on the committee, and so take an interest in the work. It's like pin money to a young lady, only if you are a proper trade union committee-man it will be spent on beer. I know quite a lot of good well-intending small-branch secretaries through this bar friendship. They stand there (at the bar), smoking their penny whiffs so that folk can see them, and say of them in an undertone of reverence, 'That's Joe Somebody, he is the secretary of the navvies' clerks.' Joe then says 'How do!' and asks you what you are going to have. Then you sup and sup and sup, and talk about who is in the union and who has run out; you switch on to 'Little Steve Bellbottom', with his big family, starting work for 'In a hurry Tom'. 'Yes; he's got in, but it's at a ha'penny an hour under the rate.' You have another sup and mutually agree he's a skunk with a lousy smell. 'No wonder there's good men walking about, Joe. Sup up and have another.'

They call themselves brothers (I should say *we*, for I'm one of them). Brothers – worthy brothers. The youngster looks with wonderment during his initiation. The shop steward proposes him, and the oldest member seconds him, then the president makes a speech of welcome. 'Welcome, little "put and taker", let's hope you are mostly a putter. Do the square thing by your fellows, always have full money and never nobstick, don't be too active, pay your contributions always. Follow the lead of the strong silent sane leadership, for remember anyone can cause a strike, but it takes a man with courage to get them back again. Still, if, if a strike happens to take place, come out and play your part.'

That I think squarely covers the mentality of most trade unionists. He wants to work as much as possible, but possesses a hazy notion that he is entitled to some scanty reward for doing it, and only when he gets to zero point does he pack up his traps. Quite a lot of branches have their headquarters at some 'Pig and Whistle'. Bonny-face, the smiling friend of all, is never too extortionate in what he charges for a club room. (Besides they often stop for an hour or so.) After all, a little fellowship and foolishness is relish for the wisest of men. John Barleycorn can make any clown become a king.

The spirit of trades unionism comes out most in such moments, intimacies are made, the jealousies and bickerings and splittings that take place on the jobs are momentarily forgotten, between cups commiserations and confidences take place, understanding and friendship is remodelled and one lives again until the job jungle monster gets you in his clutches again on Monday morning and you become once more that imperfect being – a working man.

I know you, you work-animal-trade-unionists, you want a quiet life and no trouble, but the mischief is that others want your job, they need it as much as you. You accept the principle of war for a job; may I win; all's fair in love and war. Still, worthy brothers, we have gone through long periods of slackness together, we have kidded ourselves that the man finished has been our inferior, we have wondered at times whether such statements are true, wondered if he really has lost, by losing his job, wondered if the little solvency that has been ours, the victors of the race, is worth the effort to achieve it, wondered whether our broken wind, sleepy heads and tired limbs can be compensated by the three ha'pence that stands between us and the bloke out of collar. Is he inefficient or does he possess rational thought? He is out of collar and we are out of breath. He knows life's a race of human sweat and energy, that working at the best of times is a slow ignorant way of getting a living. Still we keep in the race and will do so until by force of scientific displacement we are compelled to drop out.

Of course one reads in the yellow press a lot of bunk about ca'canny and the little shopkeeper with his grocery mind believes it to be gospel. Then there is the joke of a child mistaking bricksetters for statues, also the fable about the navvy ganger chucking up his job because he had not got a shovel to lean on, like his navvies. Ses me: that's all terminological inexactitudes. The imp of industry, the drive of the bummer, the vanity of being able to 'eat the b—— job', the need for being kept on and, above all, the recreative factors afforded by honest toil all make ca'canny impossible. The charge is about as true as the one against the tramp; you know it. The idle hobo wants the housewife's pie but not the wood-chopping; he is charged with being so lazy that if you offered him a half crown, he would ask you to put it in his pocket.

Trade unions have no rules for the encouragement of

ca'canny or shirking. They might at times try to bring about a reduction of hours, but the reason for this is the number of unemployed members on their union books. If trade is good and their members are all employed, they are only too willing to forget all about the eight-hour-day ideals and get a few more bob 'for the missus', the landlord and the bookie. I feel sure that they by their combination always err on the side of philanthropy to the poor hard-hit employers. Members of that great mass, the horny-handed sons of toil, the aristocrats of labour, from clerks to wearers of blue overalls, hard-headed men of sanity and courage, known, knowingly, the world over as that distinct type, the British working class, catered for by a hundred and one unions – examined from Mars they would look like a confusion of sections. The one big union is still an ideal, the visionaries become realists when they enter the workhouse (the only one big open-to-all union). There is a union for every little trade imaginable and if you find yourself beyond classification you can join the General Workers' Union, they refuse nobody's money. Sometimes here and there, there is a week or a month of intensive organisation by usually inert officials. This results in a gain in membership to the union organising and often a corresponding loss to some other union. They pinch and poach on one another's preserves like blazes, fighting like hell for sectional rights and lines of demarcation; the enemy at times becomes one against another and the boss is forgotten or becomes relatively a fairy godmother.

Have you ever met a trade union organiser? He is generally an ex-bench-hand. He has been like yourself, only a bit more gifted with the gab. He has generally risen to being worthy of the confidence of his mates, to be their leader, because of his fire, energy and disgruntlement with 'those in office'. From such he evolves as the pride of 'office' fills him, he becomes a mealy-mouthed speaker at meetings on the rare occasions that are sufficiently necessary to continue to justify the receipt of his ham and egg screw. He somehow loses his rank-and-file crudeness, he becomes a windbag, and one notices a touch of corpulence amidships and a desire for slumber. In the main he seems to have become a cross between a flockless parson and an overfed squire. His art seems to be confined to giving flattery and hope to the ambitious comrades, and thrashing any of the infidels who doubt his infallibility. Have you ever heard, dear reader, the trade union organiser, the parson and the squire, when faced with cross-examination by a man of capacity, how they wriggle when he gets them into a knot, then they work the old, old trick? Sez they: 'What we have to consider in this important matter is the undisclosed opinions and aspirations of the quiet man, the man who has done some hard thinking, but needs a little encouragement to draw him out, the thoughts of the meek, the man who has a very sensible opinion, but does not noisily air it, the man who is my little tame mouse, who will eat out of my hand, the man who will say yes to all my suggestions for his welfare, the man who is patient, justice-seeking, family-loving, and noted for his singleness of purpose, honesty of endeavour and devotion to duty.'

That, as you know, is sufficient to get 'Yes, Sir, them's my sentiments to a T.' So say all the meek and mild, trained and nurtured on the milk of reverence for established superiority. How people holding the reins of authority do detest the bloke who 'thinks for 'imself'! There are quite a lot of organisers in the many trade unions. It is an escape from poverty and hard work, a rung in the ladder to becoming an executive member or even to the General Secretaryship. They grumble if they have to talk shop to the great unwashed; they manage to find time to sit on police-court benches, town councils and other committees of considered social eminence. If you asked me for a definition of a trade union organiser, I would say: It's a bloke, that was once a human being, who has gone to the bad through the philanthropy of his workmates, placing him in the company of other bad men who have equally been treated with shamefully gross philanthropy, thereby becoming indolent, corpulent and consequential.

It is perhaps true that all species have their troubles. There's the English rain and the noisy slandering communists. Maybe sometime there will arise a united working class, a class that will become a wall of solidity functioning in unison for purposeless inaction, then my dear trade union organiser, as the song goes, you will have achieved your heart's desire.

There is another movement that by its activities has as much right to suffer the monica of socialism. It is the Great Co-operative Movement. The Octopus trust of working-class creation in the consumer's world. I take my hat off to the old pioneers, for their early efforts and good intent. I have in a messy sense written this poetry of a grand old school, and though it is poor it gives one some idea of their purpose.

# Fustian Forsytes

*Despite his pomp, froth and beer,*
*Man is the latest of the ephemera –*
*A pitiful creature of temperature's slime,*
*Strutting brief days upon the thermometer of time.*
*All the human drift about which we rave,*
*From cannibal down to the last slave,*
*Is but a flash, a flicker, a spot,*
*A soap bubble, a phantom, a tiny tot*
*Across the infinite sky of the stormy night –*
*'Struggling to live' sums up his plight.*
(Arranged from something read or heard,
source forgotten.)

OFTEN DO WE HEAR from the old men wheezing in the throes of asthma, 'Young folk nowadays are noan made of the same mack o' stuff as when 'a were a lad.' I have heard men of consequence come out with the same thing. 'The young men of today are anaemic and pale pink' is the summing up. Still the old boys (duffers to us) hold on, despite their infirmities, to whatever power they possess and they would feel outraged if we referred to them as being fossilised. They complain about our irresponsibility, our drift and aimlessness, our losing touch with churchianity and worshipping at the shrine of the devil carelessness. How come these things? Surely, Mr Dryfoot, if a doctor sound our hearts, lungs and sight, we pass at least presentably. Still you have the brains, haven't you, daddy? Well we have had a free education (of a sort), you paid threepence a week for yours (some sort, that too). Hang it all, what about the twentieth-century libraries, old timer? You are stepping on something that is an improvement on yourself. Don't kid yourself so much about greatness! What if we do clown about, hoike, make jazz noises on the Scotch-cum-Welsh sabbath, our age of marrying, to save good names, is higher. Our rollicking, roughneckism, short skirts and openness is an improvement on your Come-to-Jesus piety and entanglements of trollops.

What does it matter to us if you went to improvement classes and we drift to abandonment? Aren't you an old dog who has entrenched himself when there was a bit of a chance for the expression of your acquisitive tastes? Did not Victorianism, with its throb of invention, set up factories galore? Did it not allow any Tom, Dick or Harry, and even duck eggs like your uncle Ebenezer to set up shops as the gateway to nirvana? Of course there were great men then, great statesmen too. Acquisitives. Substantial, positive greatness comes of opportunity, power to do something.

Why even the old men of today will realise that the statesmen of today are 'blithering fatheads', but it is only so because they can not do something. England's day of greatness was at its peak in your youth, old sneezer, and now it's declining. So statesmen now are 'fatheads' instead of great men, and youngsters with empty hands and nothing to clutch hold of are 'indolent irresponsible pale pinkers'. Your vanity is part of the task you were set, it was a small part of the page of history. It was to make all that the world needed, and it kept you busy for some time. In the last hundred years you have done something worthwhile. You made the world rich and most people poor.

You supported the Southern States in the American Civil War; the poor nigger slave meant cheap cotton, didn't it, daddy? You suppressed the Indian Mutiny. 'But the Russians shall not have Constantinople.'

There would always be work and always be masters. You got up at three and went to your work day in and day out, since you were nine years of age too. Life was that way, wasn't it? It always would be, wouldn't it?

What does it amount to? There's an iron man now that can do as much with the assistance of a 'little indolent pale pink boy', as all the lot of you. Yes, and in half the time too. There's not much use for men now, my old stocking top, and quite a lot of the masters have gone bang too. You with your swank about the quality of British goods, British labour and big drum-beating, where are you? You have had your day because of *conditions*, not because of *greatness*.

There was a reason for your growth to exaltation and a reason now for the decline. The reason is not particularly *you* but mainly the conditions you are placed in. Take the early birds in the game of being 'somebodies': the Egyptian, Indian, and Chinese civilisations. Yes, Mr Civilised Britisher, the hen of Egypt came before the egg of England (despite our present ownership of it now, because of its ditch gateway to the other old hen, India). They, the infants at the game, became settled instead of becoming nomadic because of being Egyptian? Not on your life; but because of physical and nearly unique conditions: a Nile, plus the natural protective boundary of deserts and swamps. India and China were practically in the same boat. They could not help becoming a settled population, and thence came the development of workers (slaves) and men of culture and philosophers (idlers). Egyptian civilisation was the fruit of slaves (workers) and physical conditions. So it was with you. Your unique nearness of coal and iron made your industrial revolution, and from it grew your workshop-of-the-world, plus its awful sweating dens filled with workhouse babies and child-carrying women. The adjustment of these coal and iron properties called for women, girthed in chains doing what humanity objects to ponies doing now.

What a price is paid for topping the ladder of dominance! Still, it's an age-long story: Pyramids, Galleys, Serfdom, Factories, and now the poor slave has nowhere to lay his head, and nothing to do – so he is pale-pink and indolent. Of course when the machine displaces him, some charge must be trumped up against him, if only to shame him to a humility proportionate to his worth. Human labour power's value is diminished by society's lesser need of it; it is now scrap-iron price. Still, old timer, you made as much as you could, for consumption at home and abroad, and for production of things at home or abroad also. So long as your masters could sell they would let you make. Whatever was selling, you would be making. From that we now see our key plants, the plant that makes things, in every blinking god-forsaken country in the world.

Our imperialism has built an empire of competitors and everywhere the problem of making is so easy that anyone, white, black, or yellow, can make more than they can sell. Each can supply their own needs, each has a surplus and looks to similarly placed countries to receive their overplus (incidentally amid it all the producers and redundant working folk are eating humble pie until this problem of superfluity is solved).

Don't you see, old man, between your world of markets to flood and our new world of marketers with nowhere to market, there is a bit of difference? What we young pale-pinkers will have to see is how it is going to pan out; some say, 'Armageddon', others, 'World Commonweal'. What we can say with emphasis is, that there is going to be history made (despite our pale-pinkedness). History coming from conditions arising out of your productivity, and chaotic distribution, unfortunately we seem to be in for it.

Like all things that are to be born, there is the painful period during the pregnant progress to birth. The heart pangs of the overrated and taxed shopkeeper class, their absence of customers, due to the ever-falling wages of the real-world spending community (working pecks); the headache of the manufacturer who economises, and rationalises in order to cut, and still finds the market non-existent, the internal struggling, kicking of the child in the womb of this stifled organism, the hopelessness of continued sacrifices in the interest of national solvencies on the part of the aforementioned working pecks, the slow permanent drift towards intolerable conditions, and the ever-increasing necessity for further doses of squeezing and national economies, in order to keep the ship, H.M.S. Capital, afloating. Oh, Mr Now Fatheaded Statesman, instead of the previous glory of success and world-market capturing, you are doomed to flog yourself to exhaustion, bailing out the water of a world economic avalanche. Oh, Mr Trade Union Official, instead of praise and increased membership because of getting rises in wages, you are doomed to taunts of 'traitor' and 'sabotager'; you will be abused because you are a mere microbe in the game of transition, a transition that will show your obsoleteness and unceremoniously shuffle you off. Oh, Messrs 5-per-cent and safety-dividend-seekers, your ever-increasing pen and ink registers of assumed balances, looking for safe investment, with interest, are finding themselves more and more frozen. So it is that optimism is gradually disappearing with the ever-increasing realism of day-to-day crises, national and international.

With that we leave you, old timer, to misfortunes of funeral reform, the natural safety valve against permanence and Rip-van-Winkleism. Old age and youth cannot live together, one is yellow and mellow, the other impetuous but innocent. With us comes the bearing of the ills that are to be. As with all births, the carrier of the child gets much worse before deliverance, there is much pain and sickness, sometimes in the coming of a new babe it is at the price of the mother's life. The seasoned trickster with his dawn of a brighter morrow leaves us unmoved, we have a knowledge of society's inability to arrest the engine of production that is increasing its velocity, minus the breaks of distribution. The firemen were paid off when it had bridged the hilltop; now it is scampering down the other side.

Of course there will be a crash, but all the passengers are filled with the same thought: Will the rails, the wheels and the pilot hold on their reckless downward path long enough to see my time out? 'Can I last?' is the cry. Such is egoism in time and space. Many will be killed and many will be maimed, but from the chaos will come the drive for a 'new society'. All the inflated notions of the blue-bloodedness of aristocracy, the superlative authoritativeness of public schools' bureaucratic officialdom, the armies of grocers, canvassers, salesmen and similarly half-baked supermen, the craftsman with dignity and his lobby-house mentality, the hordes of work-animals falling over themselves indecently to keep drawing wages that will barely stop their wives from nagging – yes! all their notions, aspirations, sweetie-sweet moralities, and good intentions, will go astray. For the oncoming crash will rip asunder their very vitals, rough-hew their lives how they may.

So just as at luncheons, there are toasts, eulogies, and hypocritical expressions of mutual admiration, I a member of the 'great unwashed', must raise my mug of tea and 'roast' you all. There can be no mutuality where there is ostracism. If the Irishman is 'agin the Government' the 'unwashed' is 'agin' the whole b—— lot. Roasting thus becomes the appropriate toasting, and each toast is one commending you to eternal damnation.

Here's to you, Mr Politician. May the grandeur of your speeches and the bountifulness of your fifteen shillings and threepenny valuation of 'God's own images', be upon you in the days of judgement. May the restlessness of the desire for hearing your voice make you realise the priceless sanctity of seclusion, thus taunting you with its dignified indifference to your heavy drum-banging and molly-cosh bleatings. May you see that time is a whale and you but a sardine, and not even as difficult to swallow as Jonah. Let us hope your promises are never forgotten, your intrigues and scratchings self-afflicting.

Here's to you, Economists. Please keep up your endeavours at solvency, conduct the business of life on the 'Uriah Heap' cum 'Scrooge' cum 'Nonconformist Conscience' lines. Take off the poor here, have minor adjustments there, wrack your brains and leave the hungry more hungry with your comprehensive actuaries of lingering marginalisms. Do this, economise, make it mean what it is; the people must have less. And with it all you'll find each year of your gigantic struggle showing more serious financial problems than hitherto. Become the toadies to a system of robbers, show them the way to effect the gradual step-by-step reforms, the ever-continuing continuity of reducing the mass world people's status, get on with your job: economise, make it such a word that we, with our appreciation for words, will think it the patron saint of redemption. Each of you fall over yourself in this new fashion; it is akin to all things associated with the class mind, the robbing class psychology, 'it is wolvish, bloody and ravenous'. Its dynamic is making people suffer. You belong to the flatfooted school of perversion. You stride forward with your callous formulae of restriction, inflicting the mind with tension about problems of overproduction and, typical of your bone-headedness, you have the panacea of under-consumption.

Happiness, squandermania, glorious life to the fullness, the vast army of mothers filling up their baskets, is all anathema to you. You are the new Christ, you are full of efficiency, yet methinks we are much worse after taking your medicine. May you be compelled to drink it all yourselves and we be liberated to the extravagancies of the vineyards of the flowing cups. May we ultimately defy all your canons, may we torture you by working less, and taking more, may the added purpose of production be overcome, that is, the purpose of profit. Good old pedant, good old expert, good old economist, your continued existence will change the 'blue-eyed Saxon' outlook much more than the man on the tub with his 'froth' and his denunciation. Conquer the biological law that men will insist on being fed and then you become the supermen you claim you are.

Here's to you, Mr Parasite. You may be all right as a daddy or a philanthropist, still you're a flea, perhaps a bug. You get your living in a filthy way, you are a source of nuisance and danger to the many clean healthy industrious organisms in society. Still one has heard of fleas being removed 'without violence or disturbance'. Indian infidelism is so anti-christian that they never exterminate fleas; they even put them into silver match boxes; so does the Labour Party. Attitudes of mind can become so elevated that you can rest with your filth, safe in the knowledge of philosophy, that the gymnasts of the brain can permit a continuance of the insufferable. Still, unfortunately, only the highest of men have such a compassion and others there are who like not the bite of fleas. They being of blister and itch and irritation would like to catch and scold (some of the less sophisticated might even kill) this capitalist vermin. Never mind, old parasite, keep sucking at the good pure blood of man, there's only the match box to fear at the worst.

Here's to you, the army of heavy laden and sweaty bodies. You who are of thirst and fatigue, you who are of industry and not of ambition, inferiors, visited by the fleas, the tame mice that the economists practise their art of vivisection upon, the creators of all, the uncouth, the mugs, the seekers of jobs, the possessors of the painful quality of endurance, the dumb and inarticulate, the men of fustian, the cream of the earth, here's to YOU. Whatever I have said or writ or done, either by act or deed, in ignorance or reason, whether I sincerely believe it to be right or otherwise, and if by examination, now, or in the dim and distant future, it is found to be true or otherwise, not commendable or in your best interests, or not unduly biased in your favour, I, here and now without equivocation or qualification, irrevocably withdraw and allow you, the assaulters of the earth, the men of the horny hands, to substitute anything however alien to me in its place.

I accept you, general masses, howling mobs, beastly blondes, you are infallible, impeccable, and always right.

*What is life to me and you?*
*Is it simply drifting through?*
*Or does each moment pierce our heart*
*With throbs pulsating that makes us start?*
*Action! Struggle! and Grappling with*
*Obstacles, gives the stimulus to live.*

## VINTAGE CLASSICS

Vintage Classics is home to some of the greatest writers and thinkers from around the world and across the ages. Bringing you not just the books you already know and love, but new additions to your library, these are works to capture imaginations, inspire new perspectives and excite curiosity.

Renowned for our iconic red spines and bold, collectable design, Vintage Classics is an adventurous, ever-evolving list. We breathe new life into classic books for modern readers, publishing to reflect the world today, because we believe that our times can best be understood in conversation with the past.

*A Note on Our Sustainability Commitments*

We create Vintage Classics red spine paperbacks with the environment in mind.

We have minimised the carbon impact of our books by using low-carbon FSC™-certified paper. Our covers use minimal, reduced-carbon finishes and we are working towards making all our books recyclable. All red spine editions printed in the UK use 100% renewable energy.

For more information on our sustainability commitments, please visit greenpenguin.co.uk.

Discover more in **VINTAGE CLASSICS** red spine

| | |
|---|---|
| *Brave New World* | Aldous Huxley |
| *To Kill a Mockingbird* | Harper Lee |
| *Catch-22* | Joseph Heller |
| *Native Son* | Richard Wright |
| *The Handmaid's Tale* | Margaret Atwood |
| *The Gulag Archipelago* | Aleksandr Solzhenitsyn |
| *The Master and Margarita* | Mikhail Bulgakov |
| *Beloved* | Toni Morrison |
| *Stoner* | John Williams |
| *The Sailor Who Fell from Grace with the Sea* | Yukio Mishima |
| *The Savage Detectives* | Roberto Bolaño |
| *The Joy Luck Club* | Amy Tan |
| *Autobiography of Red* | Anne Carson |
| *I Who Have Never Known Men* | Jacqueline Harpman |
| *Oranges Are Not the Only Fruit* | Jeanette Winterson |
| *Disgrace* | J. M. Coetzee |
| *My Left Foot* | Christy Brown |
| *Sugar* | Bernice L. McFadden |
| *Death and the Penguin* | Andrey Kurkov |
| *Persepolis* | Marjane Satrapi |